DEEP DARK BLUE

Seraina
KOBLER

DEEP
DARK
BLUE

Translated from the German by Alexandra Roesch

PUSHKIN
VERTIGO

Pushkin Vertigo
An imprint of Pushkin Press
Somerset House, Strand
London WC2R 1LA

Copyright © 2022 Diogenes Verlag AG Zürich
All rights reserved
English translation © Alexandra Roesch, 2023

Deep Dark Blue was first published as *Tiefes, dunkles Blau* by
Diogenes Verlag AG in Zurich, Switzerland in 2022

First published by Pushkin Press in 2023

swiss arts council

prohelvetia

Published with the support of the Swiss Arts Council Pro Helvetia

1 3 5 7 9 8 6 4 2

ISBN 13: 978-1-78227-957-0

Designed and typeset by Tetragon, London
Printed and bound by Clays Ltd, Elcograf S.p.A.

www.pushkinpress.com

Let us make mankind in our image, in our likeness, so that they may rule over the fish in the sea and the birds in the sky.

—GENESIS 1:26

From afar, the cormorants sounded like bleating goats. He could see their metallically gleaming heads popping up where he had sunk the traps in the water. The orange storm lights were still flashing in the harbour. He was late, and the stupid creatures had taken advantage of this. The fisherman started swearing into his beard. In the past, the birds had just paused here briefly on their journey south. But for some years now, the colony had settled here. Often, when he pulled up the nets, inside them there were only two or three perch that had been gnawed on. He opened the box containing Lady Fingers, Chinese Crackers and Screech Rockets and lit several of them. He would associate the foul sulphuric stench with the birds for the rest of his life. Together with the empty nets and the incredulous expression of the employee whom he had been forced to let go after working with him for twenty years. While he hauled in the traps, he left a message with a hunter he was friendly with, to whom he paid a bounty for each shot bird. The juddering of the winch became slower and slower—something was blocking it. The fisherman put gloves over his calloused hands. The rope felt as if he had nonetheless made a good catch; eagerly he shone his light into the depths. The lamp almost fell out of his hand when a canvas shoe appeared, on a bare foot. Soft flesh, shimmering blue-violet, bulged from the bottom of a light-coloured trouser leg. He had seen a corpse once before, in the woods, many years ago. The skeletal face, with scraps of skin still attached, had crept into his dreams for a long time. He shivered. He quickly called the emergency services and was relieved to hear a human voice.

I

Ten Days Previously

I T IS SAID that that the most beautiful city in Switzerland lies by both a river and a lake. Surrounded by water that flows from pristine mountain ranges through an open valley, past densely populated shores. Until finally the city itself emerges from the blue surroundings like an apparition. And there, on the northern edge of the lake, alongside the youthful River Limmat, the medieval old town of Zurich begins.

At Chez Manon, diagonally opposite the Predigerkirche, the coffee machine started up with a hiss. Faces that were still tired disappeared behind newspapers in wooden holders until Manon served viscous espresso in pre-heated cups. A conspiratorial moment of contemplation before the shops opened and tourists clogged up the narrow streets. An ash tree towered from a nearby closed courtyard. It spread its mighty arms only when it reached the height of the roofs. At its foot was a small house with slate-grey window frames. A woman stood in front of it. She had a towel wrapped round her wet hair and was wearing a silk kimono that slipped off her shoulders whenever she bent down. Her feet were encased in earth-encrusted garden clogs of the kind you could buy in DIY stores in the country. Rosa Zambrano snapped off a sprig of verbena and was quite content with herself and the world. For the world consisted of red-cheeked radishes that were growing hidden away between summer pumpkins and broad beans, or courgettes resting in the morning sun, whose saffron-yellow flowers would soon be just right…

Instead of rowing on Lake Zurich as she usually did on her day off, Rosa was in a hurry today. She went back inside, placed the verbena sprig on the wooden table and climbed up the creaking stairs. The last injection had left a bruise on her stomach. She chose a loose-fitting summer dress from her wardrobe. This way she could get dressed quickly afterwards. A sudden whistling noise reminded her of her morning ritual. She hurried downstairs. With one hand she removed the kettle from the hob, with the other she reached for the cast-iron teapot for the sencha. A gift from her ex-boyfriend. She stopped in mid-movement and instead pushed a small stool in front of the shelf. There was a brand-new glass teapot on the top shelf. Rosa carefully placed it on the sideboard and plucked the herbs until only the purple flowers remained. After she had poured boiling water into the pot, the contents soon sparkled like molten gold. Finally, she fetched an empty ice cube tray and scattered the flowers in it, filled it up with water and placed it in the freezer. Then she gathered up the remaining stems. They too would find their place: on the compost heap.

Rosa went into the bathroom, which was in a corner of the kitchen. For a long time now she had actually been planning to convert the shed, where spiders and woodlice lived among layered firewood from the city forest, but at the same time she couldn't bring herself to banish from the kitchen the free-standing bathtub with its lacquered feet. It stood in direct line of sight of the Swedish stove, so that you could watch the crackling flames as you bathed. Like almost everything in the house, she herself had hung the mirror that she now stepped in front of. A strand of hair threaded with silver curled out of her towelling turban. She pulled a face, then rearranged her expression and smoothed blackthorn blossom oil on her cheeks and neck. Then, more out of habit than anything else, she opened the fridge and closed it again straight away: even if she hadn't been given strict instructions to turn up with an empty stomach, she probably wouldn't have managed to eat anything. She put the steaming cup of tea on the side table in the garden and sat down on the deckchair under the ash tree. Rosa leant back. The sun shone through the branches and painted fleeting patterns on her face.

2

T HE SURGERY WAS a little outside of the city in one
of those lakeside communities that were named after
the colour of the light that bathed the sprawling villas in the
evenings. As Rosa cycled out of the city, the first mothers
and fathers were already waiting at the pedestrian crossing
in front of Tiefenbrunnen station on their way to the nearby
public beach. The handles of the buggies were so heavily
laden that they would probably have tipped backwards
straightaway without the strapped-in children as a counter-
weight. Cool-bags, camping chairs, shell-shaped beach tents
waiting to be put up. Rosa wondered if all of this was really
necessary. But she didn't know. How could she? The poplar
trees swayed in the breeze on the traffic island. As did the
masts of the sailing ships anchored in the harbour next to
the concrete plant—they made Rosa think of chopsticks.
A little further on, the plastic tables outside the clubhouse
of her fishing club shone through the trees. But a glance at
her watch made her pedal harder. Beyond the city limits,
the surroundings began to change. The fences and hedges
that provided privacy grew higher, interrupted only by
heavy iron gates. Limousines and SUVs with personalized

numberplates were parked on raked-gravel parking areas. The numberplates were regularly auctioned off, bringing in several million to the city treasury each time. Rosa locked her racing bike outside a building with marble pillars and untied the fabric of her dress where she had knotted it together above her knees for the ride. A life-sized Buddha was enthroned next to the reception desk.

'Do you have an appointment?' The shrill voice was a sharp contrast to the gentle bubbling of the decorative fountain on the reception desk. The surgery assistant slid her carefully manicured hand over the telephone mouthpiece.

Rosa tore her gaze from the Buddha, whose hands were resting loosely in its lap, folded into the shape of a bowl. 'Sorry, I am a bit late.' She cleared her throat. Then she glanced casually in the direction of the waiting room to make sure that no one was listening.

'Your name?' the shrill voice asked. The door was closed. Now Rosa replied in a firm voice: 'My name is Zambrano.'

Fingernails flew like arrow tips across the full pages of the calendar. 'Here it is: Zambrano. You are here for the cryopreservation?'

Rosa winced.

The assistant crossed out the entry. 'Dr Jansen needs a moment, but the examination room is free now.' She pointed to a door at the end of the corridor before picking up the phone again.

When Rosa sat down at the large desk, she touched her ears. They were glowing and probably dark red. She shook her curls over them. She still felt the need to justify herself. Her middle sister, Valentina, was already a mother. And Alba, the youngest, was about to become one in the next few days. It wasn't that she didn't like her little niece and nephew. On the contrary, she regularly cooked for her family, or at least as often as the duty roster allowed. Nevertheless, every time, she was reminded of the void in her life by the jam and gravy stains left by greasy little hands. Alba was further away from her in age than Valentina, but the longer they were adults, the less important that distance became. And, after all, she was the one who had encouraged Rosa.

'Listen! You can get inseminated as a single woman. If you don't find anyone, then just go to a clinic abroad in two years' time. You can have everything done there. Everything!' Her youngest sister ought to know. Her partner had also undergone treatment a few months ago so that they could conceive. Successfully, as the nine-month bump that Katrin carried around like a living trophy showed. Rosa was regularly inundated with ultrasound images. Or information about how one could dry the placenta after the birth. *Try not to think about it!* She closed her eyes. She attempted a breathing exercise and gave up after two rounds. Rosa doubted she would ever learn to relax by doing absolutely nothing. She preferred to concentrate on the large prints on the wall. The door opened just as she was studying the structure of a sand dune and contemplating whether it spoke for or against the success rate of a fertility clinic to have a barren landscape adorning the treatment room.

14

Doctor Jansen's hair was a little too long considering the rest of his appearance in a white coat, although the trendy canvas shoes he wore without socks were also irritating. They reminded Rosa of the skipper with whom she took lessons for her licence for international waters. Jansen had also already crossed the threshold into middle age, but this made him even more attractive. The arch of his upper lip was curved, and the shadow of stubble was showing despite him being clean-shaven. He seemed to be the sort of person who didn't have problems, only solutions. At least this is how it had seemed to Rosa at her first appointment a few weeks ago, when he had reassured her: *Then we'll give you all the time that you need.* And showed her how best to stretch the fold of skin on her stomach to give herself the hormone injection.

'Don't get up,' he said now. He rubbed his hands routinely with sanitizer, whose scent overpowered his aftershave. He greeted her as he walked past without shaking her hand. He sat down and started typing on his computer keyboard. She didn't like it when anyone watched her type, so Rosa looked away. She noticed that the photo frame with the subtle gold border had disappeared. It had irritated her at her previous appointments because it was not facing the doctor's chair but was slightly angled, as if everyone was supposed to see how he wrapped his long arms round the waist of a woman whose red dress billowed in the wind. She had the sort of smile that probably looked identical in all photographs. The couple were flanked by two no less perfect-looking boys, who proudly showed off the gaps in their teeth. A storybook family, Rosa had thought, as her rational side briefly wondered why this put her off as much as it attracted her, even after all these years.

'I have two or three more questions. Then we can start.' Jansen turned to her abruptly. 'We can delay the process a little...' His Adam's apple bobbed up and down. 'But of course there is no absolute guarantee.'

So now he was trying to hedge his bets after all. Secretly, Rosa was glad. This put into perspective the slightly arrogant impression he had made on her. Even if it didn't change the facts: her fertility was diminishing with every day, every hour, every second with which she hurtled towards her thirty-eighth birthday. And not only her fertility: by her late twenties, most of her bodily functions had passed their peak. From the age of thirty, the probability of dying doubled every eight years. Soon her cells would lose the ability to reverse mutations. In short: she ought to have jumped on the nearest suitable man! Instead, she was sitting here having her own eggs frozen at great expense. Rosa peered at the clock. But the doctor didn't seem to be in any hurry.

'You haven't eaten or drunk for at least six hours?'

Rosa nodded. The homeopathic sip of herbal tea seemed an age ago.

'Have you ever had a general anaesthetic?'

She nodded again. And stroked the area above her knee. A few years ago, she had had a thin skin graft from her back to replace some dead tissue there. Rosa hardly noticed the scar any more. Just occasionally, when the weather changed, did the pale, bulging patch of skin itch. Suddenly she felt as if all the strength had been sucked out of her.

'Great. Then let's see if the trigger shot was successful.' Jansen rolled across to the examination chair on his leather stool. 'The ovaries of a female foetus already contain over 400,000 eggs when they are in their mother's womb. Fascinating, isn't it?' He pressed a button and the room darkened with a hum. 'But by puberty, most of them die off. Only about 500 make it to ovulation in a lifetime.'

Like the times before, Rosa disappeared behind the screen and took off her pants. Then she got on to the examination chair that spread her legs wide. The doctor inserted the ultrasonic probe inside her. A structure lit up on the screen. It looked like a bulb of garlic cut in half crosswise.

'There they are.' He pressed a little harder and pointed, not without pride, to the toe-shaped chambers. 'Seven magnificent specimens in one round.'

Shortly afterwards, Rosa was lying on a sterile examination table in the operating theatre while the assistant slipped a paper napkin under her chin.

When she regained consciousness, saliva encrusted her mouth. Her throat felt sore, as if she hadn't drunk anything for days. She didn't know where she was. With the sound of the waves in her ears that came through the tilted window, she sank back into a deliciously gentle ocean. The next time she woke up, she felt better. The IV for the propofol was still stuck in her arm. Rosa pulled her free hand from under the blanket and put it on her stomach. As she did so, she

17

thought of the missing eggs, which were now shock-frozen at minus 196 degrees, and she wondered whether a child came into being only when one of the eggs was fertilized. Or before, when someone longed for it.

'I can't possibly let you drive in this condition.' The assistant looked reproachfully at the bicycle helmet that Rosa was about to put on.

She did actually feel unsteady on her feet. She would simply push her bike, then. But the woman just didn't let up. Half an hour later, the van in which Stella drove to the local markets when she peddled her ceramics rumbled on to the forecourt. Rosa got in the passenger seat while Stella loaded her bicycle into the back. A small, scented tree dangled from the rear-view mirror next to a small dreamcatcher. Rosa felt sick.

'Let's go, I can't leave Suki alone for too long,' Stella said as she pushed the empty dog basket alongside the bicycle. 'You are quite pale.' She walked around the van and handed Rosa a bag of ginger sweets.

'Alba hasn't lost any weight,' Rosa mumbled as she popped one of the sweets in her mouth. The paper crackled as she crumpled it between her sweaty palms and formed it into a ball. Her friend was only a year older than her, but she had always known that she didn't want children because above all they meant one thing: dependency. On the way back into the city, Rosa told her what she could no longer keep a secret. And hoped that it would not cause too much trouble.

3

One week later

H E WOULD HAVE WISHED for a different ending. A final version with a love that glowed as bright as Perseid meteor showers in the August sky. A love like a summer's night in which life exploded—and everything is stronger, heavier and warmer. But he didn't manage it. Although he was still working on it on his deathbed, Giacomo Puccini, creator of the most famous operas of his time, left behind nothing but a stack of scenes that did not make up a whole: *Turandot* was to stay fragmented.

Now one of the arias thundered out of the speakers, as tall as a man, hidden under panels of fabric to the left and right of the huge screen. *Nessun dorma*! Night of decision. 'No one sleeps,' ordered the murderous Princess Turandot. She set a challenge for each of her suitors. And executed those who didn't pass.

Moritz Jansen breathed in with the swelling voice of the tenor, as if it were possible for him to take all of this in forever. The heat from the sun that was stored in the stone parquet of ancient quartzite. And the joy that tickled his legs in the form of Alina's toes, with their crimson nails. They were sitting in the middle of the spacious square that spans the edge of the old town between Bellevue, the lake and Theaterstrasse. On their blanket were the remains of their picnic, which had consisted of stuffed vine leaves, goat's cheese and a baguette.

The opera house rose up in front of them in the light of the spotlights that shone for everyone to see. Angels with outstretched wings watched over them from the roof, along with deities in flowing robes, with swords and swans. Around them on the square were lots of people sitting on camping chairs they had brought along, on damp towels or simply on the ground. Alina poured the rest of the sparkling rosé champagne into the two crystal goblets. She had bought these at the flea market, together with the lilac silk dress, which looked a bit like the sort of dress you would imagine wearing to the opera if you had never been before. It touched him. And she looked ravishing in it. Usually when they met she wore sneakers, loose-fitting jeans tucked into striped socks, and some sort of top that didn't get in the way beneath her lab coat. With pointed nails she opened her handbag, which had no handles. Her flatmate had explained to her that a clutch was a must with off-the-shoulder dresses and had lent Alina her own. Alina's face lit up in the glow of the screen as she sprinkled the MDMA crystals—finely ground for this purpose—into the champagne, which was now no longer cold.

'It probably tastes disgusting.' She raised her glass. 'Good times guaranteed though.' Then she swirled her glass, slowly and carefully, until the liquid was also spinning in circles. She took a sip. Jansen downed the bitter sediment on the bottom in one go. It was not the first time they had taken something together. But it was the first time they had done it when they weren't alone. He wanted nothing more right now than to lay her down between cool sheets. He leant over towards Alina, so close that he could touch the sensitive spot on her neck, and asked if she wanted to leave. He loved her smell. Citrus peel with a hint of green wood, mixed with clean sweat. He would be happy to miss the rest of the third act; written by a former pupil who had put together, with sugary pomp, the scenes left behind by his maestro. Too much Alfano. Not enough Puccini.

He placed Alina's high heels neatly in front of her. The shoes had been lying some distance away; she had removed them with relief two hours earlier. Then he shook the bread-crumbs out of the blanket and laid it round Alina's bare shoulders. Hand in hand, they crossed the busy Seestrasse and walked along the promenade towards Utoquai, out of town. Alongside the barriers that were already set up for the half-Ironman the next day. It felt good to walk through the night with his secret girlfriend, who would now no longer be secret. And the following Monday they would be heading for the mountains for a few days.

From further and further away they could hear the final applause for the public opera, the sopranos, tenors and chorus now bowing on the radiant balustrade above the crowd. A film of sweat had formed on Jansen's top lip. Everything was soft and fluffy, blending with the music that filled him, together with the intoxicating feeling that comes over you when you pass from one world to another and realize that your inner state and your outer environment finally match. How is it possible that you can find yourself in exactly the right place at exactly the right time—and in the right company? Laughter wafted through the air, light and round. His own or that of others, all was one. Waves swelled back and forth, not only on the nearby shore, but also in Jansen's ears. *It wasn't possible,* a thought flashed through his mind.

'Puccini could never have come up with the ending,' he said. His jaw clicked as he released his impending lockjaw with a deliberate jerk. 'It would not have been possible to finish the opera. Not as long as he himself—like the prince in his story—desired the wrong woman,' he added. He touched the spot where until recently his wedding ring had been.

Alina looked out across the lake. 'Have you spoken to your lawyer again?'

Ships with lighted lanterns swayed like fireflies further out. For a moment, Jansen thought he had spotted a motorboat he knew only too well. He had wasted two hours of his life on it that very afternoon. He was annoyed, but only for a moment. He no longer depended on it. On her power games. And certainly not on her. Then the *Panta Rhei* slipped behind a shadow and was simply obscured by the railing of the largest excursion ship on the lake, encircled by cold blue lines of light. Jansen squeezed Alina's hand even more tightly. It felt strangely hot and cold at the same time. At least he would hopefully be able to settle things with the woman who was still his wife. Even if Alina doubted that twenty years of marriage could be squeezed into an amicable contract. At the beginning of the relationship, she had been convinced that he would disappear again one day and go back to his wife. Ever since he had been trying hard to convince her of the opposite.

'Moritz? Did you hear me?'

'The lawyer... of course, I will call him,' he replied, and the pressure in his jaw immediately built up again. 'But not until we're back from the mountains.'

People were sitting on the edge of the quay wall, under trees and on benches. Gathered in groups around portable loudspeakers from which music blared. Many different styles, and yet: all the same and all commercial. But that didn't bother Jansen, not today. Someone jumped off the jetty with a low cry, there was a splash. They lay on their backs on the grass. Alongside them plastic cups of iced tea, fogged up by cold. When their mouths felt too dry, they rolled to the side over the damp dew, drank in long gulps and enjoyed the goosebumps that spread over their whole bodies: *cutis anserina*, one of the most exciting examples of the connection between the central nervous system and the skin that was already forming during embryonic development. He heard Alina crack the melting ice cubes between her teeth. The screen on his phone was still black. No message. When Alina placed her head in the hollow of his shoulder, he felt her nipples through the fabric and felt himself getting an erection.

Everything was spinning when Jansen got up a moment later. He pushed his hair out of his face; he hadn't had it cut since they had been together. Then he patted down his jacket, feeling for the memory card hidden deep inside the inside pocket. Ready for the public. Ready for the journalists that he would contact as soon as they got back from the mountains. Until then he could hide the card in Alina's room, where it would be safe. Shortly afterwards, the outline of a villa emerged from the shadow of a tall beech tree. Bow-fronted, a façade of hewn sandstone squares and tower-like soaring chimneys lent the building something mysterious. Even more so in the gathering clouds. Treetops brushed restlessly over the scene. Shutters slammed. Glasses clinked somewhere. Further back, lightning flashed, where the Alps unfolded above the lake and the Vrenelisgärtli glowed on fine evenings.

'I think they are all asleep already.' Alina, wrapped in the picnic blanket, was trying to unlock the entrance gate—not succeeding at first. She pressed an index finger to her lips. Giggling, they entered the imposing hall that opened on to the garden, darkened by cedars and yews. The heat of the day still hovered indoors. It smelt of the cut flowers that stood in a tall vase on a small table in the entrance. Dahlias, hydrangeas. Asters. The ballet studio with its polished floor lay silent. At first, Alina had only taken dance lessons here to improve her posture, which had been affected by all the standing in the lab. Then the opportunity had arisen to rent a temporary room in the large flat-share. It was at the top of a winding staircase, which they now crept up. A bushy-haired cat lay on the sofa and raised its head indifferently when they quietly opened the door. Light from the street shone through the stained-glass window, transmitting floral patterns on the light-coloured cushions. 'Shoo!' Aline didn't like pets. Maybe the cat knew that. Maybe it just wanted to show her that it had been here longer than Alina. The cat strolled in a leisurely way across the shaggy carpet towards the door and rubbed itself provocatively against Jansen's calf.

'Scotch?' Alina lit some candles. Jansen wrapped his arms round her waist from behind. Biting her earlobe, he felt desire rise up in him again. She gently disengaged herself and went over to the drinks trolley, which stood in front of a wall full of pictures. Petersburg style of hanging, she had explained to him when he first came round. A variety of frames close together, round and square, from tiny to mirror-sized. There were scientific sketches of animals, a giant auk, butterflies, the skull of a rhinoceros. In between there were snapshots: mother, father, daughter and son—in changing constellations and chronology. Landmarks of memory as found in all family albums, with which one assures oneself of one's own existence. But most important to Alina seemed to be the picture that was placed in the middle. It showed the Earth floating in space. A green-blue hemisphere, veiled by clouds, rising behind the moon. Taken by an Apollo 8 astronaut whose mission was to search for the moon—and who found the Earth in the process.

Ice cubes clinked as Alina placed the heavy-bottomed glasses on the travel trunk that served as a coffee table. 'Earthrise,' she said, following his gaze. 'It may sound overly dramatic, but I want the picture to remind me every morning when I get up and every evening when I go to sleep that we are only guests on a tiny cosmic oasis. In the middle of infinity.'

'I rather wonder why we didn't meet each other much sooner?' Jansen said, and pulled her in close again.

Alina placed her naked thigh on his lap and replied: 'Maybe because I would still have been almost a child?'

He groaned theatrically. Then he allowed his hand to slide up the inside of her thigh.

'Seriously...' Alina said. 'Just a hundred years before this picture was taken, Jules Verne wrote about three adventurers who had themselves shot to the moon by cannons—and who came back down to Earth with parachutes. Pure science fiction, back then.'

Jansen leant back further into the sofa; he enjoyed the taste of smoky peat burning down his throat.

'That is as if we were to imagine travelling to another solar system today,' Alina continued.

He guessed what she was getting at: 'Or as if our species would begin evolving according to its own rules. In its current form, *Homo sapiens* would be nothing more than a stopover on a never-ending journey to a complete existence.'

'Then sex would be purely for relaxation...' Alina said. She put his glass down and took off his shirt. He could see himself reflected in her wide-open eyes. His lips only brushed hers at first, but soon became more insistent. They moved across her armpits and navel, down to the soles of her feet. Jansen suddenly realized that he could never have expressed this kind of sexuality the way he had been before. But now everything fitted together in an almost perfect way. Alina spread her legs as he laid her on the pillows. Without taking his eyes off hers, he sank down on to the carpet. When his tongue found her clitoris, she slowly began to move her pelvis. He inserted two fingers inside her, just the way she liked it, and she took over his rhythm...

When she came, he was flooded with a love and vitality that dissolved body and soul and perhaps even time.

4

THE REVOLVING BRUSHES of the municipal cleaning truck droned much too loudly for a vehicle
that was barely longer than a bicycle. The noise grew
ever louder. Ever more unpleasant. Eventually deafen-
ing. Rosa swerved and rode across the street to the riverbank. By Bellevue Square, the view opened up to the
lake, in which a glowing morning was reflected, herald-
ing another blisteringly hot day. Rosa actually loved this
time of day in summer when it was already bright but
the city's inhabitants were still in a deep sleep. But the
stench that rose to her nostrils didn't quite fit the image:
a pungent smell of urine mixed with that of spilt beer.
On the Riviera, a long flight of steps that lined the bank
of the Limmat in front of the Quai Bridge, lay crushed
beer cans and half-empty liquor bottles with contents
that were yellow like nicotine stain. A half-eaten kebab
was drying in a pool of cocktail sauce. Normally, at this
time of day, the city was so clean that you could have
walked barefoot, but the thermometer hadn't dropped
below 20 degrees for the last few nights. There had been
some trouble around the lake basin. Stabbings, robberies

and altercations between groups of drunks. Hence the surveillance cameras in sensitive areas, with signs pointing them out. The previous evening, an Opera for Everyone performance had attracted thousands of people. The event was part of a wider campaign to raise public awareness of the Zurich Opera House.

When Rosa had heard that *Turandot* was to be performed, she really wanted to go. Perhaps because the World Cup, which had made the opera world-famous, was one of her best childhood memories. They had set off in the middle of the night for the South of France to visit her maternal grandmother. Rosa lay wrapped in blankets in the back of the car, her younger sister's soft breathing drowned out by the steady hum of the engine. That summer was the first time she had eaten artichokes. She had dipped the hard leaves in mayonnaise and pulled them between her upper and lower teeth. Afterwards she bathed her fingers in a bowl of lukewarm water with lemon slices floating in it. In the evening, the streets, bars and gardens were buzzing and cheering as the matches were broadcast on flickering television sets. And like thick vanilla ice cream dripping from a cone, *Nessun dorma* floated above it all. Luciano Pavarotti not only sang it to open the tournament, he also stormed the charts with it, the first person to combine the high culture of opera with the appeal of pop music. The song was playing on the car radio as they drove along the beaches with the windows down, holding their hands out into the oven-hot air…

Although Rosa liked the festival atmosphere on Sechseläutenplatz, she couldn't bring herself to go out into the crowd on the evening of the performance. But she hadn't needed to anyway—like almost all big events in the city centre, the sound had carried *Turandot* at a pleasant volume all the way to her garden, the myth-enshrouded Black Garden, where she had listened over a Campari Orange, her legs propped up.

The lake lay in the morning light, gentle and wide. In the eyes of some, it was the only thing that gave the banking city anything like profundity. For at the bottom of the lake the city was freed from being a city, and at its deepest point its depth was still seventeen metres greater than the height of even the highest tower. Glistening spots glided across the surface of the body of water, which lay under a cloudless sky. Still slightly out of breath from the fast bike ride and the even faster change of clothes, Rosa rubbed the inside of her swimming goggles with a little spit. There were hardly any waves. The ships, turbines and motors didn't start to arrive until there was no wind. She still had a bit of pain in her abdomen. But the cramps of the first days after the operation had quickly subsided. Relieved to be able to resume her training, she walked down to the shore. She needed the outdoor exercise. 'Something happens to you when the space you are in is infinite,' her father used to say. He had made that the touchstone for all his decisions, even more radically

since he had retired. Most of the time he lived in an unheated forest hut on the Uetliberg. Her mother, however, wanted nothing to do with it. She thought that this was the very thing, among many other things, that had made Vincent a terrible husband. Rosa, on the other hand, could understand him very well. Her own modest perspective on the world widened a little with each day she spent outside. That was one of the reasons why, as a young history teacher, she had stopped teaching, when she had barely even started. One of the many things her mother couldn't or wouldn't understand.

After just a few strokes Rosa's body merged with the water, which was clear and transparent near the shore. The lake did not have *one* colour, it had *many* colours. There was the churning bottle-green after lengthy summer rains. There was the bright, foaming slate-blue during spring downpours. And a dull slate-grey on very foggy days in November. There was the azure blue under a brilliant blue autumn sky when, all around, the colours were richer and fuller than usual. And there were many, many more. Among them this shimmer of turquoise blue when the algae retreated to the deeper water in summer. Rosa could make out swarms of fish against the wave-shaped sandy bottom, possibly rudd or perch. The steady, repetitive movements of her body, carried by the water, slowed the flow of thoughts in her head. She experienced the same state when she was cooking or on walks and hikes, when thoughts began to sort themselves as if by magic. She thought of Richi.

'He's completely different from anyone I've ever met,' he had enthused over the washing line a few days ago. Rosa hoped that he would not be disappointed this time. She took it as a sign of seriousness that Richi had managed to keep his romance to himself for so long. Maybe she could bake a *tarte tartin* when the two of them came for dinner tonight with Stella. There was still some sour-cream ice cream in the freezer...

Soon Rosa was completely absorbed in the rhythm of her own breathing. But the calm of the lake was deceptive. Beneath its surface, there were fresh killings every day. Just a few strokes away from the walkers and bathers who would soon make their way to the arboretum, the catfish lurked immobile in the shallows. It needed neither light nor eyes to find its prey; its sensitive barbels were all it required. When a coot was in the right position, the catfish would spring up and break through the surface of the water with its mouth wide open.

5

MORITZ JANSEN was standing on the balcony of the room where his mistress was sleeping. *I'm sorry about yesterday. Something came up, something important.* If he was completely honest with himself, he had been expecting this message. Burning paper crackled softly as he inhaled the smoke. A half-moon was fading in the sky. The phone vibrated twice more in quick succession. *I know now how we can come to an agreement. But it's urgent. Can we meet? I'm on the boat.* He put the device away, only to pick it up again immediately afterwards. The battery indicator was blinking although he was only communicating via the encrypted programme. *Head out to the buoys in front of the lighthouse,* he typed and then switched the phone off completely. It wouldn't take long. An hour maybe, two at the most...

Soft-footed, he gathered up his clothes, which were spread on the floor around the box-spring bed. Alina's eyelids fluttered a little, but she did not wake when he kissed her goodbye. Then he felt the back of the picture frame again and made sure that the curvature of the cardboard backing did not give away his hiding place. He didn't dare to turn on a light until he was in the bathroom. While he buttoned up his white shirt, which was no longer so white after the interlude in the meadow, he looked in the mirror. The night had not yet left any traces on his face. On the contrary, it was luminous. Alina had simply reprogrammed a world he had thought to be unalterable, overturning laws with the same ease with which she brought together molecular biology and action art in her performances under a sky of dancing points of light, to spherical music she had recorded herself. He hoped he would be back before she discovered the note he had left on the pillow just in case. She would think he was only in the surgery for a few minutes, which was true in a way. Then he quietly closed the door and got into the taxi that was already waiting for him in front of the house.

The property, which had access to the lake, was surrounded by a brick wall. Jansen paid the driver, who was already being summoned to the next job by a discordant voice and hurriedly accepted the cash he was holding out, which generously rounded up the amount he owed. The marble columns, previously swallowed by the pale morning light, flashed brightly as the motion detector caught Jansen. Further out, the outline of a motor yacht was visible. Should he go straight down to the boathouse? It was a good two hundred metres to the buoy. A swim would be good for his circulation. But then he remembered: toxic blue-green algae had been spreading for days, right on the shoreline. She wanted something from him, so he decided that he could take his time. Jansen headed straight for the entrance to the practice to have another coffee and get changed before paddling out.

Once he arrived upstairs, he dropped on to the Corbusier couch. As he put his head back he realized how tired he was. Alina purchased the crystals from a retired chemist. Top-quality stuff. Too pure, actually. He mustn't give in now. Continuing as before was not an option. His decision was irreversible. Professionally as well as privately. He had already cleared the air weeks ago with the woman who was still his wife. Although she probably didn't see it that way. At least the letter from the district court, which still lay unopened on the designer sideboard in the hallway, spoke to the contrary. 'You have made a fallacy out of my life,' Ellie had said at the end of the—obviously failed—mediation. He had then moved into the converted studio under the roof of the practice; the kitchenette was still unused. The only thing he used regularly was the espresso machine, which the cleaning service polished to a shine every week. He either had food brought by the Thai delivery service or had a snack on the terrace of the Hotel Sonne, which was not far away. He hadn't packed much from the family home into his weekend bag: a few books on Zen Buddhism, an ebony statuette and his clothes. Once he had made up his mind, it took him less than thirty minutes. His diplomas and photographs were already hanging in his office in the practice. He saw his sons every Sunday if they weren't at holiday camp, as they were now. They went to the cinema together or went out on a rented pedalo; he bought them ice cream, popcorn and sweet drinks and then took them back to their mother. He thought about the offer for his shares in the start-up in Zug. If he played his cards right, money would not be an issue. At least not yet.

A quarter of an hour later, after a quick shower, Jansen left the studio. He was now wearing clean linen trousers, a fresh shirt and a blue sweater that he had tied round his shoulders. The waiting room of the practice was lit only by the pale glow of the aquarium. Guppies with neon-blue and flame-red tails floated in the water. The childless couples who came to him often had a long struggle behind them. The seemingly inseparable pair constellations in which the fish swam around seemed to encourage them. There was no need to tell them that these were fish of the same sex that came together again every morning. Behaviour that humans considered friendship.

At the jetty under the copper birch, he lowered the tiny dinghy into the water, climbed in and picked up the paddle. The stillness of an early summer morning still reigned on the water. They had often met out on the lake, which allowed for discretion. Jansen could imagine what was coming, but his mind was made up. Wind rustled in the reeds. Reflexively he looked back to the shore, which threw him off balance for a moment. But he kept paddling, even though the plastic floor on which he was kneeling began to sway. The memory card was safely hidden in the villa. Later he would bring it to Alina in bed with a breakfast tray: freshly squeezed orange juice, coffee, a bag of still-warm croissants from the bakery—and the genetic code. He had the chance to make it accessible to people. All people! Not only those who were like him. What a world they could create...

At first Jansen didn't notice the dinghy capsizing. The water was barely colder than the sweat on his forehead. He lost his bearings. Swam down, rolled back to where the first rays of sunlight were shining through the surface of the water. He got tangled in the thick carpet of seaweed and his phone slipped out of his pocket and disappeared. When he looked up through the blue-green water, he saw a figure in a dark wetsuit coming towards him. She moved more like a fish than a human being. Her feet had turned into a single wide fin. Mirrored diving goggles with a wide field of vision covered the upper half of her face. He panicked. She dived after him. A stab in his leg. Another one. Neoprene hands on his ankles. Heaviness pulled him down. His senses blurred. He saw the sun, naked, bright and glaring. When he closed his eyes, Alina appeared to him. Their first encounter on the dance floor, the unreal light of the strobes and her body: a perfect melody. Then the images flickered, a whole life squeezed into a few seconds. Highs and lows, connected by a ribbon of memory that floated freely and lightly through time and space. The crumpled faces of the twins, dozing on his naked chest after the birth, his fingers enclosing their tiny hands. He felt his own mother's rough hands on his wet forehead as if he had a fever. Then he breathed out. His lungs felt empty. Water flowed through his auditory canal, pressing against his eardrum.

The last thing Moritz Jansen heard was the rhythm of his heart, like a distant vibration that slowly died away.

6

Rosa's wet swimming things dripped on to the changing room floor. Her boss had had the room built specially a few years ago when Rosa joined the force at Forellensteig, the first woman ever to do so. And that was despite the chronic lack of space in the simple pavilion that had been put up more than eighty years ago as a temporary measure alongside the boathouse. Parts of the lower floor were regularly flooded when they had high water. Nevertheless, Rosa preferred the weathered police station to any new building. The polished wooden floor reminded her of ship planks, and when she sat alone in the incident room she felt as if she were on the bridge of a deep-sea steamer. The building was surrounded by a belt of reeds, from which, now that it was July, there came trilling and chirping sounds as though they were in the jungle. They had been waiting for Georgina to spawn for days now. The 1.8-metre-long catfish could be mistaken for a small shark at twilight, except that she only had blunt plates at her disposal to crush her prey—mainly fish, but also pigeons or the occasional duck. There were horror stories about a dachshund being eaten, but it must have been a very, very small dachshund… The wild foreplay during which Georgina was driven around the nest in wild loops by her partner was breathtaking. It sometimes went on for hours until Georgina was able to free herself, in order to sink down one last time to leave her eggs behind before she disappeared. It was said that she spent her nights under the terrace of the historic wooden baths at the Utoquai—which was why so few fish ever ventured there any more.

The smell of freshly brewed filter coffee came from the service kitchen. Rosa hurriedly threaded the holders on to the belt of her uniform so she could attach her service weapon, torch, radio and handcuffs. She gave herself the luxury of having her work clothes washed and ironed by a specialized laundry service. It gave her more space at home. But that wasn't the only reason. Some of her uniformed colleagues had frequently been spat at, insulted and threatened on their way to work. These reactions reflected the difficulty of the job: police officers had to make split-second decisions on the spot, without being able to deliberate for days or weeks like politicians or judges. Their tasks usually had a direct constitutional relevance, which did not necessarily contribute to the popularity of the profession, even if the maritime police were liked a little more.

It was almost six o'clock by the time Rosa hurried into headquarters with a regretful look in the direction of the service kitchen, where the coffee would have to wait a while. Fred was an old-school boss. He had a sort of internal operating plan with a few select rules. But you had to keep strictly to them. The most important one: everyone had to be on time for meetings, in summer and winter, no matter how stormy or rainy it was. The second most important one: loyalty. Both internally and externally. And it was as easy and as difficult as that. Rosa grabbed her tablet and arrived just in time. Tom had been on night shift. He pushed a mug of hot coffee over to her, which she gratefully accepted. The display showed a water temperature of 21.2 degrees. It would go up to 22 by the evening, with light wind from the north-east: almost perfect conditions for Georgina.

Quite a number of reports that Rosa had been putting off for the last few days were piled up on her desk. This was not because Rosa didn't like writing them. On the contrary. But she feared that the formal language that she had to use to write her protocols would rob her of the last remnants of style she had left after her studies and academic writing. When she was feeling motivated, she tried to insert a personal touch to her reports, as far as the narrow framework allowed. And her motivation could usually be increased with hot coffee. She had a good hour before the first triathletes started around the lake basin. A group of sporty amateurs had initiated the Ironpeople a few years ago, after the Ironman had been moved from Zurich to the Bernese Oberland. The shortened Ironpeople course, which was much easier, attracted more people each year.

'Ship adrift,' Fred's voice boomed through the corridors. He had taken over the cockpit from Tom. 'Possible missing person.' He didn't need to say any more. Rosa ran over to the dark-blue metal rack where sports bags and plastic boxes were stored. She stopped in front of the sign with her name on it. You never shared your diving gear in the maritime police: it was like life insurance. Although Karim was listed as the frogman today, they both had to be ready to dive at any moment. A few moments later Rosa boarded the *Principessa*, the water foaming at its stern. The maritime police had to go out time and again because of boats with no one at the helm. Most of the time the reasons behind it were harmless. A mooring mistake. Rough water. But the call from a stand-up paddleboarder out near the chocolate factory sounded worrying.

Karim throttled the engine down and allowed the *Principessa* to drift alongside the teak-clad yacht. Rosa was able to tether the two boats together. A short distance away, an older man with sporty sunglasses and washboard abs sat on his board.

'Seven minutes. Not bad,' he said glancing at the non-existent watch on his wrist, and fastened the waterproof bag in which he carried his valuables. 'I paddle through here every day. When I came through on my morning round just after six there was nothing there. Something is not right.' He pointed to the stern of the boat, which bore the name *Venus*. The lounge, with its cushions and rumpled blankets, lay in the shade of the high-strung canopy. A bottle of champagne was upside down in an ice bucket, next to two used glasses. Straws that had been cut into pieces, a partly smudged line of coke.

'I'm going on board,' Rosa said, and put on some latex gloves. The motor yacht swayed in the oncoming swell of the first passenger ferry headed for Bürkliplatz. The instrument panel was lit up. But more importantly, the motor was still running at idle, which had also puzzled the stand-up paddleboarder, who clearly also felt responsible for keeping order on the lake. While Rosa switched off the ignition on the *Venus*, she heard Karim dictate the yacht's registration into the radio before he got ready for the dive. They both knew it was going to be difficult here at the deepest point of the lake. There was an almost empty Ziploc bag on the table, which Rosa put into an evidence bag for examination before it got carried away by the wind. She flipped over a plastic card that seemed to have been used to crush the powder. However, it was not a credit card as she had hoped, just a voucher for a multiplex cinema.

'We need to try to restrict the area,' said Karim, pointing to the empty pilot's seat and the blue jumper that had got caught up in the swim ladder and was partly hanging in the water. They quickly radioed headquarters and asked for backup. Rosa knew that they shouldn't allow themselves to be fooled by the pleasant morning atmosphere. Most people drown without calling out or flailing, but rather silently, almost secretly. Their lungs fill with water. The concentration of water molecules rises and rises, faster and faster, until it is higher than that of the surrounding cells. Then the water molecules enter the red blood cells, more and ever more, until they burst.

In fact, the lake was too deep at this point for Rosa and Karim to make it to the bottom. They had to turn back after forty metres. They had no other choice but to take water samples at various depths. They didn't know yet whether they were dealing with a crime scene, but if they were the evidence had to be collected as soon as possible. The yacht had been moved to the boatyard at Forellensteig, where it was being examined by technicians in protective clothing. Although most crime scenes contained countless traces of DNA, not every genetic fingerprint belonged to a perpetrator. The trick is recognizing the relevant traces. Two champagne glasses, one of them with lipstick marks, seemed to indicate that there had been more than one person on the *Venus*, at least for some of the time. The local police were already on the way to the owner of the small motor yacht, who had sounded eminently alive on the telephone. And he wasn't missing a boat. Rescue service helicopters had been circling overhead since midday. Rosa wiped beads of sweat from her forehead, not taking her eyes off the monitor as she did so. In contrast to sunken vehicles or ships, a drowned person was often only visible as a faint echo. Thanks to the combination of thermal imaging cameras and the echo sounder, it was nevertheless possible to scan the seabed systematically. Rosa had arranged for all fishing nets in the surrounding area to be pulled in. Without success. They were searching for the proverbial needle in a haystack.

A clap of thunder cut through the heat-laden air above the lake. For days now, thunderstorms had been approaching in the late afternoon, but so far it had never amounted to more than a few distant flashes of lightning. Either way, they would have to break off the search by nightfall at the latest. Rosa thought of Romeo and Julia, as they had called the elderly couple. The two of them had been swimming one evening, which they did regularly, as their neighbours and children all testified. The cramp in her leg had taken the woman completely by surprise. Her husband had seen her flailing her arms in shock—and tried to save her. He had drowned in the process. And then, as soon as she was back on dry land and recovering, she had suffered a heart attack. Romeo had disappeared without a trace. For months they had searched for him whenever they had some free time. They had grid-searched the area.

Rosa actually found the lake comforting. Each of its waves hid the insight that we only rise up against infinity for the duration of our short lives—only to subside again in a gentle wave. And to merge into a world in which no matter is ever lost, only changes its form. But when the depths swallow up a person just like that, then this image loses its comfort.

They did eventually find Romeo. In a completely different part of the lake. And only by chance because of a sudden change in the weather. But Rosa would never forget the gratitude in the eyes of his children. They were only a little older than she was. In the months following the accident, they hadn't had the heart to bury their mother's urn alone. Their parents had been inseparable for more than fifty years. And during the crippling wait, something inside them had frozen too that only released when they knew that the two of them could be laid to rest together again. Since that experience, Rosa had developed a kind of affection for the sight of the dead who were found in the lake. They did look disfigured when they were brought up from the depths, but she liked them a thousand times more than the corpses you usually encountered in the police service.

7

T HE WAY BACK to the city centre was like a sluice. With every metre that Rosa cycled in the shade of the trees in the parks, she got a little closer to normality. People queued up in front of ice cream vans, the smell of bratwurst permeated the air and teenagers sat listening to reggae music in a circle in the Arboretum. Flags from the public holiday advertising the Ironpeople and Opera for Everyone still fluttered from the trams, while the city's cleaning service had already removed the remnants of the two major events. Rosa was always impressed by the speed with which everything was dismantled. But this was just child's play compared to what would take place a few weeks from now when the Street Parade boomed around the lake.

The walls of the apartment building on Rindermarkt were as thick as monastery walls. They kept it cool in summer and insulated in winter. A few American tourists were standing in front of it, enraptured, taking pictures of each other with the date that was engraved above the door. Then they stroked the sandstone lintel, as if they needed to make sure it was real. The notion that this building was already here before their continent even appeared on the world map clearly impressed them. Rosa smiled and unlocked the door. Gratefully, she took in the subtle smell that greeted her. Regardless of the time of day you entered the house, it always smelt of the same mix of yellow soap, beeswax polish and the paints belonging to the antique furniture restorer who had a small shop on the ground floor. He didn't just sell furniture, he told stories. The shop window was his stage, which he set in the same way he ran the shop: sometimes funny, sometimes political, but always affectionately with a certain sly humour. The window display changed every few days. One of its most famous displays consisted of fifty white Easter bunnies and one brown one looking the other way. Many in the neighbourhood came by specially to gain inspiration from the collector's items that had been restored, some with secret compartments, even though it was not worth repairing them—unless you also took into account the value of feelings.

Instead of taking the wooden stairs to the upper floors, Rosa walked to the end of the hallway, where daylight fell through the pane of glass set within the solid oak door and secured with ornate wrought iron. Her heart still leapt when she walked down the stone steps into her garden, the Black Garden.

The hurly-burly outside the façades of the medieval row of houses intensified the peacefulness of the sheltered back-yard. The gravel crunched under her steps—a sound that belonged to the yard as much as the Gothic window at the entrance and the uneven roof terraces of the surrounding

48

houses. The traces of time had overlapped and reassembled for so long that they made a unique patina. Rosa dropped her bag on the ground in front of an iron table, sat down and slipped the shoes off her swollen feet. The *tarte tartin* wasn't going to happen. It was too hot to eat anyway, let alone to heat the oven. Instead she would smoke the whitefish that had been marinating and serve it with a watercress salad and onion-raspberry jam. And as a starter, homemade rye crispbread with salted butter and her grandmother's recipe for cold soup. A scoop of ice cream to finish. If anyone was still hungry afterwards, there was soft cheese and fig chutney in the fridge.

A little later Rosa stood barefoot on the terracotta kitchen tiles. She and Leo had brought the tiles back from their holiday in Provence and laid them themselves. Between the exposed beams on the ceiling was fastened a piece of string on which bunches of camomile, mugwort and valerian had been hung to dry. The beams and the entire house dated back to the Middle Ages, as evidenced by a copperplate engraving from that time. Rosa happened to come across it in the city archives when Nelly was still alive—long before she moved in herself. She had been examining the reformers' views on witchcraft for a project paper. The sources did not indicate that Zwingli and his fellow Protestant campaigners had given much thought to black magic and covens. But Nelly—always reading several books at the same time, and full of curiosity until the very end—had been delighted with the reproduction of the engraving and had hung it above the coat stand, where it was still to be found. Even if the little house looked completely different now.

When the doorbell rang, Rosa was in the process of caramelizing finely chopped onions and sugar with red wine. She wiped her hands on the apron that she always wore tied round her hips. Then she pressed the buzzer for the entrance door on the other side of the row of houses. Heels clattered on the flagstones, in unison with the scrape of paws. Thanks to Suki the beagle, you could hear Stella's approach long before you could see her, as the animal had an impressive range of sniff and snuffle noises.

'We were in the area. Shall we go off for another walk?' Stella came towards her without awaiting Rosa's reply. The flowered layers of her skirt, which she had paired with a leopard-print shirt and several strings of wooden beads, fluttered as she walked. It didn't matter what Stella wore, it always looked as if she had simply pulled the things out of her wardrobe haphazardly. And yet the combinations of patterns always harmonized in such a way that you wondered why everyone didn't wear them. Although it was probably more down to Stella than to the prints. In contrast to her striking appearance, her face was completely bare. She only used soap and water, no powder, no eyeshadow, not even mascara.

'Definitely not, come in.' Rosa pushed her friend gently towards the kitchen sofa. She placed a bowl of water on the floor for Suki and tossed her one of the grapes she had picked out for this purpose. The dog snatched her favourite food out of the air with flopping ears and thanked Rosa with a look that translated as: you and me forever. At least until the next grape. Rosa took the bottle of *Räuschling* wine, which she had bought at the bodega a few days ago, out of the freezer compartment.

'Almost perfect,' said Rosa as she uncorked the wine with a dry plop.

'Have you heard from him?' Stella indicated towards the cast-iron teapot that had been banished to the shelf. Leo had given it to Rosa during their semester together in Japan.

'He took the job in the Foreign Office. I think he's with the embassy in Algiers at the moment, but I don't know for sure.' Rosa craned her neck, whereupon fine furrows formed on her brow which immediately disappeared again, as if the nerves were having a tug-of-war for control of her face.

'I almost forgot,' Stella said, and placed a small package on the table. It rustled as Rosa opened the newspaper the package was wrapped in, causing Suki to rub her wet nose expectantly against Rosa's leg. Two handmade matcha bowls appeared.

'You actually did it.' Rosa held up one of the bowls and admired the colour gradient, which moved from red jasper to matte black. Stella told her how the fire alarm had gone off during the first firing attempt and two fireman in full gear had suddenly appeared in front of her. In contrast to normal ceramics, the Japanese *raku* technique produces heavy smoke when the red-hot pieces are removed from the kiln with tongs and then turned in hay. Rosa hugged her friend. Pretty much everything in Rosa's kitchen was either made by Stella or bought back from trips. Everything except a misshapen bowl, Rosa's first and last attempt at the potter's wheel in Stella's studio. She used the monstrosity anyway and collected stones in it that she got out of flower beds. As a kind of daily reminder to herself that she should focus on just a few things, but do them properly.

'Are you fully recovered from the procedure?' Stella gnawed clean the pit of an olive and sympathetically raised the thick eyebrows that gave her a hint of Frida Kahlo.

Rosa thought of the diminishing pull in her lower abdomen and made a dismissive gesture. 'It was nothing. I am much more concerned about today's search operation.'

'I saw when I took Suki for a walk. Still no luck?'

'Unfortunately not. And we had to stop the search when it got dark.'

Stella speared another meaty olive, which was seasoned with finely chopped preserved lemons. 'Completely off-topic—but is there vermouth in here?'

'Just a dash of Noilly Prat,' Rosa said.

Stella rolled her eyes enthusiastically. Then she carried on. 'It's a bit creepy though. I mean, theoretically, the body could wash up anywhere at any time.'

As often in the past, Rosa was torn between the wish to confide in her friend and the constraint of her obligation of non-disclosure. Suki pushed her floppy ears forwards and tilted her head. Then she started to wag her tail. Richi could not be far off. Sure enough, two men appeared in the garden moments later. Their hair gleamed as if they had just showered. Rosa thought that the heat suited them a lot better than it did her.

'Something smells delicious.' Richi handed a pot to Rosa, who was coming towards him. Lemon-yellow fruits bobbed on dark green leaves. He knew that she could make much better use of a Aji Lemon Drop chilli pepper, classified as an eight on the Scoville scale, than a bunch of flowers.

'*Capsicum baccatum*! Richi! How did you get your hands on such a rare specimen?'

'To be honest, Eric found it.' With that, Richi stepped aside and introduced them to each other. Then he went into the kitchen, where he was greeted loudly by Suki and Stella. Eric ducked his head when he followed in behind.

'It's all right once you're in.' Rosa pointed to the kitchen ceiling. 'This used to be the district wash house. But there are only two rooms, including the kitchen.' She filled more glasses with white wine and flower ice cubes and handed them to the new arrivals, who looked as familiar with one another as if they had known each other for much longer than a few weeks. All Rosa knew was that Eric had studied abroad and had now taken a position at the university hospital. Richi seemed so relaxed around him, as if he had been released from a constraint. Who knows, maybe Eric was exactly the man that Rosa had wished for her best friend.

Eric and Rosa had grown up in the old town together. That sounded idyllic, but they had both carried a carefully guarded feeling of strangeness that was part of their child-hood, like scraped knees on cobblestones. Back then, there were a lot more children in Niederdorf than now. A whole gang of them met up in the mornings at the Nike fountain. The imposing school building on Hirschengraben, with its ornaments and turrets, could have come straight out of a fantasy epic. Elaborately carved wooden figures with wrinkled faces and protruding eyeballs and nose rings sat high up on the walls of the panelled assembly room. 'Racialized heads,' as a historian would later write in a report commissioned by the city: stereotypical features underlined by matching fur hats and jewellery. At the time, no one had bothered to reflect on these witnesses to a past in which people and other living beings were ruled by classification. Only the caretaker, Mr Greco, climbed up a high ladder once a year and cleaned the faces, first with a damp cloth, then with a dry one. Richi felt distanced from the other children from an early age, something he had no words for, until one of them asked straight out why Mr Greco didn't wipe his face too.

Recently, Rosa had come across a Brazilian artist who firmly believed that nobody was black and nobody was white; she had made it her goal to document the true colours of humanity. According to her system, Richi's skin was not caramel or milk chocolate, but straightforward Pantone 66-3C. Although this was not quite true because the delicate freckles that covered his nose and cheeks were a shade darker.

8

THE WOMAN WITH a sports bag on her back arrived at dusk. Bats whirred through the air, chasing insects. A wall of black-grey cloud built up above the lake; there wouldn't be much time. She slowed down and parked her racing bike by the patchy yellow grass area. She kept her helmet and gloves on. Her quick strides grated on the sandy path. A few youths were smoking weed on the jetty, but at the far end of the park, by the weeping willow, it was quiet. She looked around several times. Then she pushed her way through the branches. The lush green cave-like spot was almost invisible from outside and stretched almost five metres over the water. She breathed a sigh of relief when she saw the bag dangling from the tree trunk. With a practised motion, she untied the rope and packed everything into her sports bag. Waves slapped on to the shore. A small boat with an outboard motor approached. She quickly pressed herself against the broad tree trunk. But it chugged past her towards the harbour. Then she shouldered her bag and went back. Fire bowls were burning outside the diving school as they did every Saturday after training. Someone was strumming a guitar. Glass holders with candles in them stood on the tables. An all-too-sweet smell of vanilla drifted over from the chocolate factory. Some children were playing hide-and-seek nearby, shrieking loudly. This was the moment she had been waiting for. She slipped in through a back door near the toilets. The course room was empty, and she slipped silently to a wall where the school's diving equipment was stored. There was a zipping noise as she opened the sports bag. She replaced the monofin. Voices suddenly approached from outside. Two men with shell necklaces round their necks, badges of the recently completed certificate, walked past the course room to the kitchen. Beer bottles clinked against one another when the fridge was opened. 'There was a bottle opener here somewhere...' one of them said. 'Wait, I'll take a look in the course room.' Steps sounded in the corridor. She froze. 'It's all right, mate, I've found a lighter,' someone called from the kitchen at the last moment. 'That works just as well.' Bottle-tops popped. The footsteps turned back. Shortly afterwards, the woman with the sports bag swung herself on to her racing bike, which sported a small sign with a number and the logo of the Ironpeople under the seat.

9

R OSA STEERED HER GUESTS outside for the aperitif. Earlier, she had placed bowls of olives and semi-dried tomatoes, marinated feta cheese and smoked almonds on the table, which she had decorated with a dark tablecloth and bunches of dried lavender. 'You have to try the tomatoes, they grow right here on the side of the house,' Rosa said, and retreated to the kitchen.

The jam in the saucepan glistened turnip-red, the raspberry seeds cracked gently between her teeth and the whole thing had a balanced sweetness with a slight aroma of violets. Rosa seasoned it with a pinch of salt before filling a jar with the lukewarm mixture. Then she fetched the large bamboo board and the knife—not any old knife but a Miyako knife with a hand-forged steel blade. She had bought it in a Japanese factory in Seki which had been producing knives, as well as Samurai swords, for more than seven hundred years. At first Rosa had worried about her fingers when she diced things. Since then she had mastered the thin, matchstick-like batons that were ideal for the wok. As she had made the gazpacho the day before, all she needed for the cold soup, made according to her Yaya's recipe, were some chopped peppers, cucumber and tomatoes. Then she took the filleted whitefish out of the fridge. While she put two large saucepans on the hob and spread the dry-smoke mixture of juniper berries and black tea on the bottom of the frying pan, she listened to the conversation through the open window.

Stella was trying hard not to pester Eric with the usual 'What is it that you do?' questions. Instead, she engaged him in a conversation about the difficulties of finding a flat in the city. She did it so cleverly that she did actually manage to learn quite a bit about him. For example, that he was currently living in a boarding house above a trendy coffee shop in District 4 and had grown up in a small German town close to the border. Rosa carefully placed the fillets of fish, which had been marinated in sugar and salt, on the two steamer baskets and switched the flame to medium heat.

When the smell of smoked black tea wafted through the kitchen, Rosa poured the gazpacho into the soup terrine with the domed lid and dark-blue ornaments. Only rarely did Rosa plate up her food in individual portions. For one thing she considered it patronizing, in culinary terms, if she decided on the portions people got; plus, she didn't want to see someone forced to eat certain things out of politeness. She also hated it when edible leftovers ended up in the bin. When all the dishes and bowls were filled, she carried the tray out into the garden and was greeted with joyful exclamations.

'Do you have your own boat, or don't you fish?' Eric dabbed the corners of his mouth, which were actually clean, with the cloth napkin. The gesture gave Rosa the impression that he wanted to show her that she had his full attention.

'Unfortunately not, although the boat wouldn't be the problem...' As she spoke, she followed Richi's gaze and passed him the fish platter. 'It's just that it's almost impossible to get a mooring near the city in the span of a lifetime.'

'Not even when you're with the maritime police?'

'Not even then.' A strange buzzing noise sounded through the branches of the ash tree. It was quieter than the search helicopters that had been rattling in Rosa's ears all day, but irritating nonetheless. Clouds had gathered, but the muggy air still made her thighs stick to the chair.

'But I am lucky...' Rosa continued. 'A friend of my father's occasionally lets me use his yawl. Hey, do you guys hear that too?'

'I hate them!' Stella pointed across the roof terrace of the flat diagonally opposite the wash house. A drone was buzzing in the direction of the Zürichberg. 'Do you think they are filming us?' Stella picked up her wine glass. She was one of those people who always heard, saw and felt more than she could process. Sometimes an overly loud conversation at the next table was all it took. If the views expressed during this disturbance also went against her principles, she quickly lost her composure.

'If I am not mistaken, that is medical transport,' Eric said. He told them about a trial at the university in which tissue and cell samples were transported by drone. A clap of thunder shook the walls of the house and brought the

59

conversation to an abrupt end. Shortly afterwards, when the dull-grey sky was dissected by lightning, they were sitting in Rosa's kitchen eating sour cream and peppermint ice cream. The spicy smell of summer rain wafted through the open door.

'I wonder if the drone was storm-proof? Who knows what it was transporting? It makes me think of that crazy guy.' Stella poured the last of the *Räuschling* into their glasses, leaving out Rosa, who indicated she didn't want any more. 'Did you hear about him? He grew human hearts in monkeys. Now he wants to use them as donor organs. Completely perverse.'

'Hydra. Typhon. Chimera. Children of the underworld.' Richi liked to use the baritone of his theatre-trained voice—as well as his stage German—whenever a conflict loomed or he wanted to protect himself.

'I mean it!' Stella got up. She began clearing the dishes, very loudly. It wouldn't be the first time the two of them locked horns after a couple of glasses of wine. Interestingly, they got on really well when they were alone. Sometimes Rosa thought the two of them only fought to see whose side she would take.

'Ah, come on… that's a comfortable position you are speaking from.' Richi got up and helped her fill the dishwasher. 'You would be grateful for a donor organ if you needed one. Or would you rather die?'

Suki hid behind the bathtub when Stella replied, incensed: 'We will die, eventually. You, me, him, her, it—all of us. That's part of the game. What right do people have to play God?'

Rosa drew patterns with her spoon in the puddle of ice cream on the bottom of her plate, then she looked up: 'You mean like I did?' She pre-empted what Stella would have come out with any moment now anyway. This way, at least, Richi heard it from her.

'Oh come on, that is *completely* different.'

'Why? I am also creating artificial options for myself.'

'What have you done?' There was a hurt undertone in Richi's voice. Rosa thought of the pact they had made more than two decades ago when they had both been sorely shaken by heartbreak for the first time. If they were still alone by the age of forty, they had sworn they would start a family together.

'Rosa must tell you herself,' Stella said, throwing the kitchen towel on the sideboard. Then she sat down on the floor with Suki, leant against the bathtub and let the wooden beads of her necklace run through her fingers as if she were praying a rosary.

'Can we agree to settle this bilaterally?' Rosa asked, and pushed her chair back as if she wanted to remove herself from an invisible line of fire. Then she leant her head against the wall.

'You could see it this way,' Eric said diplomatically. 'Basically everything—from hand axes to copper celts to in-vitro fertilization—is an intervention in nature. From the moment our ancestors first picked up a tool, humans have been challenging nature. And continue to do so to this day.' He remained silent as he reached for the water jug and refilled their glasses. 'But you could also say that humans, their tools or their in-vitro fertilization are just as much part of nature as birds and their nests, ants and their mounds, foxes and their burrows and so on. So why—why on earth—should we not strive to improve our lives and our species? Or, to put it differently: would it not be almost our sacred duty, given the state we have put this world into?'

10

T HE FISHERMAN was sheet-white under the dripping hood of his oilskins. He was standing so that he had the winch with the half-pulled-in net behind him and didn't have to look. A violent thunderstorm had whipped across the lake during the night. The waves were still quite high, but were becoming calmer. Empty petard shells rolled across the deckand there was a smell of burnt Lady Fingers in the air.

'How am I supposed to get back to shore?' he asked, and crossed his arms.

'By taxi boat,' Rosa replied patiently.

The relief was evident in his face. When he was picked up fifteen minutes later, he was repeatedly assured that the maritime police would return his ship to the harbour as agreed. After the sound of the taxi boat's engine had died away, Rosa climbed back on to the large salvage vessel to Tom, who was preparing for the dive.

Rosa followed Tom on the screen from the salvage vessel's control centre, glad that the site was not deep. Below the thermocline, the water temperature drops rapidly with every metre until it reaches the bottom of the lake, where it remains constant at 4 degrees. In some cases, they had no choice but to rake the bottom of the lake with a construction of razor-sharp barbs and long ropes and to then pull a body up to a diveable level. This was not possible without causing postmortal injuries.

'I need paper,' Tom shouted. There was not much of him to see in his diving gear. Rosa went to the boarding ladder and handed him a waterproof notebook with coated pages and a pen dangling from it and, in return, was handed several tubes with water and sediment samples.

'Are they still not here?'

Rosa, also in a wetsuit and ready to help Tom with the upcoming rescue, shrugged her shoulders. The report had gone to the public prosecutor's office shortly after the fisherman's call. An emergency investigative fire squad team should have arrived a long time ago. The term 'fire squad', used for a mixed deployment of specialists in 'burning events' such as capital crimes, hostage-taking or serious accidents, dates back to the early days of the local police. But it seemed that the team in charge had just been deployed to another mission, so the standby service had to be called in. Rosa had the shuttle boats diverted. These brought in commuters—who were able to combine duty with pleasure over a coffee in the on-board restaurant—from the lakeside communities to the city centre. Not a time at which one wants to witness the recovery of a victim of drowning.

'Finally!' Rosa says. They can see the *Principessa* coming into focus in the distance. There are three more people on board alongside Karim, who is at the helm. Shortly afterwards they join Rosa on deck.

Inside the salvage vessel, prosecutor Andrea Ryser—with trouser suit, pearl earrings and light-coloured eyebrows that made her subtly made-up face look even more bare—pointed to a monitor and gave Rosa and Tom final instructions before they both dived down in a swirl of bubbles. She would then keep in contact via radio. The body was caught upside down in the nets. Rosa and Tom approached with the underwater cameras. A long, slender body, clearly male. His shirt glowed strangely in the green of the lake. Tom attached signs with numbers where the net was torn.

Ryser had brought them up to date as soon as she arrived: 'It never ceases to amaze me. How can someone just disappear unnoticed in this city?' No matching missing-person report had been filed by Monday morning. The maritime police had suspended their search on Saturday evening. The owner of the *Venus*, on the other hand, had come clean when he learnt the details of the incident. He did rent out the yacht and the mooring site—without permission, because he spent most of the year in the South of France; otherwise, however, he wanted nothing to do with the matter. The sub-tenant was a posh establishment in Niederdorf, not far from the central library. There you could rent a yacht with 'companion' for the appropriate cash amount. The owner of Neaira had been quite cooperative, Andrea Ryser reported, but according to her the boat was not in operation on the evening in question. The laboratory findings had been more fruitful: they had found ketamine on the boat, a substance that was originally used as a narcotic for horses in veterinary medicine but which had become increasingly popular on the party scene because of its hallucinogenic side effects.

They got closer and closer to the body. The dead man's facial features were discoloured, the skin on his hands very shrivelled, like when you have been in the bath for too long. Forensics might not be able to get any fingerprints. The arms were twisted inwards and stiff, the thumbs clawed into the palm. Rosa wrapped the body in plastic with Tom's help, first the hands and head, then the rest. When she noticed the canvas shoes on the corpse's bare feet, an image flashed through Rosa's mind that she immediately dispelled. Instead she concentrated on the recovery, with care and caution, because the dead body should not be injured any more than absolutely necessary. And if a crime is suspected, this principle applied more than ever.

T HE FORENSIC PATHOLOGIST had a hunched posture, his head slightly bowed, as if he didn't dare
straighten up completely or direct his gaze somewhere
where the others weren't looking. Right now it was an
examination table they had set up in the materials room at
Forellensteig. Simon Fisler carefully opened the body bag,
from which lake water was still dripping, and cut open the
trousers and shirt. He mumbled to himself, repeating the
findings as he typed them into the laptop he had brought
along. Rosa felt responsible for the dead bodies recovered from the lake. At least while they were with them at
Forellensteig. Even if their story was a blank at this point
in time that could only be filled later with dental records,
X-rays and DNA analysis, Rosa regarded the remains of
a body as having become something that someone took
care of. Had to take care of. First at the coroner's office.
Then at the crematorium. Finally at the cemetery. Until
there was nothing left of a life but memories and a few
handfuls of ash. And maybe a grave that would be cleared
in an orderly fashion after twenty-five years and rented out
again. Rosa wondered what the dead doctor's body would

tell them. And what had made him get so stoned that he had an accident like this.

In her mind's eye she pictured the photo on his desk in the surgery. The picture-perfect family. The sunset, the sea. People with an addiction problem often had two faces. Always trying to keep up appearances, they created an image of themselves, put it in a gold frame and reproduced it so often that they themselves believed this was them. Until everything collapsed: intensely and uncontrollably.

The actual autopsy would be carried out later in the institute; the inspection of the corpse was limited to an initial examination of the body with the forensic pathologist only documenting external injuries. There were quite a few of them, because the current had dragged the body across the stony bottom of the lake after death.

'Can you see the livor mortis?' Fisler pointed to dark spots that could be seen all over the body. 'As soon as the blood is no longer kept in motion by the heart, it submits to gravity. It sinks to where the body touches the ground. At least usually.'

A succession of clicking noises could be heard as he photographed the dark spots. 'But in this case, the vessels were compressed from all sides. The blood wasn't able to collect in one area, but spread under the pressure that the water exerted from all sides.'

'Which would mean the man didn't die on land but in the water,' Rosa concluded.

'Exactly.' Fisler covered the body with a sheet. 'That will be all for now from my side.' He closed his suitcase.

Immediately after arriving at Forellensteig, prosecutor Ryser had gone into a meeting with Fred in his office. Rosa's suspicions weighed heavily on her; she would speak to her boss straight away, before the forensic pathologist went to too much trouble identifying the man. But there was something else.

'Is there any coffee going?' the fire squad officer who had accompanied the rescue asked as he looked at Rosa in her tight-fitting wetsuit. It was the first time they had seen each other since the police academy. Instead of a uniform he was wearing shorts, a hoodie and running shoes. Otherwise, however, Martin Weiss had hardly changed: steel-blue eyes flashed beneath wavy hair, which he still wore in a side parting. He had the ability to lend his gaze a depth into which you could always interpret a little more than was perhaps meant. He had confused Rosa more than once with it, in a not unpleasant way.

'Down the corridor, turn left.' Rosa pointed her hand in the corresponding direction, which she immediately realized was a completely unnecessary gesture.

'Did I tell you that you have barely changed, Zambrano?' He beamed at her. Blood was pulsing in Rosa's head. She grabbed a cylinder of compressed air. 'Maybe we'll see each other later. I need to sort out the equipment now.' She took the stairs to the changing room, while he walked past her with a spring in his step. She stopped halfway down.

She looked back. Martin was leaning against the kitchen doorframe, looking at her and smiling.

'Why didn't you mention this before?' Fred drummed a Biro impatiently on the table.

'It didn't come up before.' Rosa shifted a little in her chair. 'Besides, I am not completely sure…' She didn't mention how embarrassed she was.

'When did your sister undergo treatment there?'

'To be honest, she wasn't the only one.'

'You're pregnant?'

'No. Well… no! But I would like to be. Perhaps, at some point…' Rosa felt she had to apologize because they both knew that this would be the end of her service at Forellensteig. Fred nodded and tidied up a couple of loose pages lying on the desk, as if he needed a bit of order.

'Why does a successful gynaecologist hire an escort?' he asked after a while.

Rosa shrugged her shoulders. She had had the same thought. 'As far as I know, he was married. But it's the right price category.' She found it offensive that someone who spent all day gaining intimate insights into the female psyche would then pay women to be compliant after work. Not only because she was his patient herself. But also for that reason.

'Take the afternoon off,' Fred said as if he had read her mind. 'I'll take care of the rest.'

L EO HAD ALWAYS CALLED IT 'North Korea boot camp', Rosa recalled two days later as she was working out. It would actually have been difficult for her to explain what the fascination was with doing a workout with close to four hundred bodies, densely packed in a large gym, where most of the time you were within range of someone being able to kick you in the backside or, if you took a wrong step, you might end up being the kicker. Perhaps it was down to the absolute presence that you needed in order to become part of this sweaty crowd. Rosa had remained loyal to the Academic Sports Association after she had finished her studies. And from the many hours she had spent here she had drawn the inner certainty that you could learn (almost) anything if you repeated it often enough, because movements, like habits, inscribe themselves into the body and make it something that goes far beyond its original abilities. This made the idea of having a date that same evening all the more unnerving. Martin Weiss had written to her shortly after the operation. A situation she had not been able to prepare for in her seventeen years at Leo's side. During their training, Martin had also been in a steady relationship. She had considered the tension she felt in his presence back then as a purely physical reaction: pleasant, but meaningless.

Now it was different.

There were many beautiful views of the city. But when Rosa climbed the stairs to the Polyterrasse and rose a little higher above the city with each step, almost out of its midst and yet hovering above it, her heart swelled each time. However, after her training today, it was almost impossible to get there. 'Genetic Science Days' was written on a banner stretched over the magnificent rear entrance to the Swiss Federal Institute of Technology (ETH). A stage had been put up in front of the three high double doors of the Semper Building, named after its architect, which filled the entire space between the two golden candelabras. A group of students stood in front of it holding up cardboard placards and painted banners that shimmered with heat: 'Open Science, Open Thoughts', 'Set Our Books Free!' or 'Giants on the Shoulders of Giants'.

Up on the stage, in front of the abandoned lectern, a demonstrator stood with a megaphone in her hand: 'Who owns science?' she shouted to the crowd. 'We do!' it echoed back from there. It was lunchtime, people were standing under awnings in front of stalls and street food trucks, there was lentil curry, poké bowls, even a pizza oven on a cargo bike. Rosa's gaze returned to the main ETH building. Someone had stuck Post-it notes on the inside of the windows in the shape of oversized keys, with angry emojis next to them.

Rosa remembered reading something about the protests by young scientists against current research conditions. Because in the natural science disciplines, often only well-known institutions and state laboratories could afford access to the scientific evidence. Even students at renowned universities had only limited ability to study results and the associated data.

A female security guard came on stage, while her colleagues moved the barriers to create a wide aisle to the audience. She was followed shortly afterwards by a man with oval glasses. The trousers of his dark-grey suit crinkled at his ankles. The excess material there had come from his middle, where his shirt strained over his stomach. The man, presumably one of the vice-chancellors of the university, cleared his throat, a sound which was amplified by the microphone that was already switched on.

'Ladies and gentlemen... no city in the world has more Nobel Prize winners than Zurich,' he proclaimed. This was followed by a very high-pitched microphone screech. Rosa reflexively covered her ears. She turned aside and looked for her bike, which had to be somewhere among all the other bikes that had arrived since she locked hers up in the parking area that morning. She quickly realized that it was hopeless. She would have to fetch it when the event broke up. On the way to the steps that led down to the old town, Rosa came across a mobile molecular kitchen; it had emulsified lemon foam in petri dishes and wobbly raspberry-coloured pyramids that probably didn't taste of raspberries, lollipops with liquid content and rainbow-coloured drinks in test tubes.

'What can I mix you?' The student behind the counter wore a lab coat and a transparent face mask with rhinestones stuck on it. He had a disposable cap over his long hair. Rosa ordered a drink with little spheres that looked like caviar. She thought of her mother. There had been a time when she had been totally obsessed with eating at El Bulli. And when she set her mind on something, she usually managed to do it. And so the day arrived when she put on a silk scarf, got into her rickety Renault 4 with a friend, blew a kiss to her daughters, who were ten and twelve at the time, and headed off to Spain. To the lush bay on the Costa Brava, overgrown with gorse, rock roses and wild thyme, where haute cuisine had been reinvented in a nondescript, chalky-white building. Back in Zurich she had experimented for weeks, although she never usually 'cooked' more than a few fried eggs and sandwiches for her daughters. Alba and Valentina shovelled slippery lakes of soup, tortellini filled with fruit and fermented cheese into their mouths with infantile enthusiasm. While Josefa, with her wooden spoon raised in the air, explained to them that molecular cuisines required a kind of creativity that could not be achieved without precision and order, Rosa dropped the disastrous lumps into the toilet. She knew that precision and order were things that did not necessarily correspond to her mother's impulsive nature.

'It's not the strongest species that survives.' Rosa could still make out what the vice-chancellor was saying from back here. 'It's also not the most intelligent.' After a pause for effect, he continued: 'But the one most willing to change.' His gaze wandered briefly over the crowd, then lingered on the demonstrators. 'These are not my words. No, the quote is from none other than Charles Darwin, whose *On the Origin of Species* is undoubtedly one of the most scientific works ever.' She noticed that he spoke the same statesmanlike Swiss German that some of the federal councillors on television did. She sucked at the thin glass tube that was stuck in the salmon-coloured spheres. Green tea. Jasmine. Balsamic vinegar. And a bit too much sugar. But nice and cold.

'When we talk about change, then we have to speak about the CRISPR/Cas process. Nine letters that perhaps contain the greatest opportunity of the twenty-first century. For *Homo sapiens*. For humanity. For us!'

A gap opened up in front of Rosa and she moved forwards a bit, out of the scorching midday sun and into the shade of the building. There were only spheres left in her cup now. They felt like a bubble bath in her mouth. When she pushed them against the roof of her palate, they burst and spread the taste of ripe honeydew melon.

'Two names usually come up in this context: Jennifer Doudna and Emmanuelle Charpentier are considered to be the inventors of the process. They were awarded the Nobel Prize in Chemistry just a few years ago. But there is a third name that is almost as important. We are proud to have a brilliant and progressive researcher in this field teaching here at the university. Please join me in welcoming Professor Marie Duval.'

75

A woman detached herself from the background and walked purposefully towards the lectern, where the vice-chancellor stepped aside to applause. When quiet resumed, she said in a clear voice: 'Imagine that cancer had become curable. The mother of all illnesses. Disappeared. Just like AIDS and most hereditary diseases… but are we allowed to do everything we are able to do? This is the question we want to discuss over the next few days with the involvement of the wider public…'

If the vice-chancellor had done a good job of hitting the tone of Swiss politicians, then Marie Duval was the UN Secretary-General. Her body language was just as stylish as her appearance: cognac-coloured wooden sandals and culottes with a classic blazer and an overlong bob that was very slightly tousled in the right places. Rosa's thoughts stopped in their tracks. Her date! She looked at her watch. High time. She had no idea what she was going to wear that evening. She made her way through the crowd. She was already on the steps when she heard the speech being interrupted by jeers. The demonstrators from earlier were on the university roof. They had taken down the Genetic Science Days flag and were hoisting their own, with a stylized key depicted on it. No sooner was the flag fluttering in the wind than the security guards arrived. But the few minutes were enough to capture everything on camera. They didn't need more than that; the real power of the action lay in the pictures. They would surely flood the internet that same afternoon.

13

R OSA CYCLED ALONG the languidly flowing river. The sun was burning, although it was already above the wooded ridge behind which it would soon sink. She got off her bike at the Love Bridge, as the locals called the narrow footbridge, which crossed the Limmat in front of the main railway station. The railings were barely visible under the many padlocks. Groups of tourists planted themselves in front of it and took photos with selfie sticks. Rosa had always found it a bit silly when she watched couples attaching the *lucchetti dell'amore*. As if love could be captured by writing your name on a padlock with a waterproof felt-tip before casting the key into the river in a ceremonial act to sink to the riverbed forever, or until the next dredging. When Leo surprised her with a golden padlock after their last trip to Florence together, she was nonetheless delighted. *Rosa & Leo, per sempre.* He had even had their names engraved on it. At the time, she interpreted this as the long-awaited commitment to start a family. They broke up shortly afterwards. A few days later—as her first act of unwanted freedom—Rosa cut through the lock with a bolt cutter from the station at Forellensteig. Afterwards she threw it into the nearest public waste bin, which did actually make her feel better. At least for one evening.

The restaurant that Martin had suggested was on a narrow strip of land on the River Sihl just five minutes from the hustle and bustle of Bahnhofstrasse, where the monthly rent for a square metre of shop space was more than double Rosa's salary for the same period. Colourful lanterns lit up the riverbank promenade, whose embankment was overgrown with waist-high rushes. She used to come here a lot in the past, because Richi studied in the same building. Every inch of the wall was covered with colourful absurdities. An oversized skeleton squinted down at her from the high ceiling. Rosa was a little early. She went to the toilet, ran ice-cold water over her wrists and pressed them against her neck and temples. When she returned, Martin was already standing at the bar, where beer was being served between luminous plastic Madonnas. He had swapped his sports gear for a white singlet and jeans rolled up to his calves. Summery Havaianas flapped on his feet as he walked towards her.

'Do you want a beer too?' He kissed her on the cheek while running his hand down her spine, which immediately triggered a shiver that Rosa enjoyed on the one hand but which she found overwhelming. Knowing that anything she could say now would only be superficial chit-chat to disguise her confusion, she nodded silently when Martin suggested they go outside with their two beers. She had soon successfully steered the conversation to work. Martin told her how the CID had changed in the last few years. He was sensitive enough not to bring up anything that might have touched on the events that led to Rosa getting the scar on her leg. When he brought up the current case, Rosa almost choked on her beer. She put the bottle down.

'Are you quite sure?'

'The blue-green algae in his lungs were unequivocal: there is no way the dead man could have gone overboard at the spot in the lake where the motor yacht was anchored. There are also no standard drowning findings such as severely overinflated lungs. It seems more likely that his breathing had already been restricted.'

Thoughts were swirling through Rosa's head. 'Does that mean he didn't drown?'

'Yes, he did drown. We found diatoms in his bones and organs but he also had a colourful mix of various psychoactive amphetamine derivatives and alcohol in his blood. A large dose of ketamine probably finished him off.' Martin paused and drank a bit too quickly from the bottle, and some beer foamed on to the table. He wiped it away with the back of his hand and carried on. 'Or put differently: if Jansen hadn't already drowned, then toxin-induced respiratory paralysis would probably have caused his death.'

'I wonder who was with him? After all, he can't have steered the boat to the chocolate factory himself. Possibly a panic reaction on the part of his companion?' Rosa speculated.

'In fear of being suspected? Maybe. He would have been easy prey in his state though,' Martin said, and drained his beer.

Rosa thought of the woman in the gold frame who had disappeared so suddenly from Jansen's desk. Did she have something to do with her husband's demise? The most cunning crimes usually occurred in the home environment. Rosa was briefly tempted to tell Martin about her connection to the dead doctor. But only briefly. She intentionally drank her beer slowly. 'It would be really useful if you knew where he had died,' she said. Her gaze was drawn to the entrance of the pub where a poster was hanging showing the young Diego Armando Maradona. He was wearing a T-shirt with Che Guevara on it. An icon on the chest of another icon, so to speak.

'That's why Ryser was with your boss today,' Martin said. 'Do you know anything about blue-green algae? It's really fascinating.'

Rosa actually knew quite a lot about it, but she was curious to know what it was that fascinated him so much. He told her how delicate threads floating in the sunlit water aeons ago had had the effect of destroying an entire world that had previously been a warm, peaceful ocean. When the threads started to produce oxygen, they wiped out all living creatures that were not adapted to it. And laid the foundation for today's world.

While Rosa listened, she was amazed once more by the strange turns life sometimes took: these primeval blue-green algae,which had once caused mass extinction in order to make another world come into being, were now uncovering the potential murder of the man who, in a way, was supposed to be at the beginning of the life of her potential child. Perhaps it was similar to the icon on the chest of another icon: an eternal recurrence of the same.

'There is no way you can get a hangover from that,' Martin said. He held the glass at a slight angle and slowly poured tonic water into the gin. Rosa's doubts about the gin claim showed in her voice as they toasted once more, but the longer she looked into Martin's face, the stronger her feeling of knowing him became. She didn't know much about him. Just that he'd had a passion for vintage cars back at the police academy. And for the kind of women who had to cloak themselves in a mysterious aura to distract from the fact that they were actually unstable, which is why they always took advantage of those men who were good to them and idolized those who treated them badly.

'Have you never thought about coming back?' Martin snapped her out of her thoughts. He turned his empty glass back and forth between the palms of his hands.

'Coming back?'

'Yes, to CID.'

'Never.'

'Why not?'

'Because I'd much rather look at the lake than into the depths of humanity.'

When Martin offered to get another round of drinks shortly afterwards, Rosa insisted that it was her turn to pay. Martin was willing to accept only on the condition that the next round was on him again. And the longer they sat under the colourful lanterns, the louder the crickets chirped in the grass, the lighter Rosa felt. She rarely drank more than one glass of wine with dinner. Alcohol did have a loosening effect at first, but experience had shown that it was downhill from there. Today, though, she decided, today would be different!

Rosa was sitting on the toilet. Despite her bladder being full, she couldn't get a drop out. She heard Martin moving glasses around next door in the kitchen. He opened the fridge but didn't close it again, as if he were looking inside like someone who didn't know what he was looking for. If she could hear *him*, then he would surely hear *her* too. It was only when she turned on the tap and the splashing sound in the sink drowned out the sound of her stream of pee that relief came. She washed her hands. And couldn't resist the temptation to look in his mirror cabinet for possible traces of a woman. The bottom shelf contained camomile mouthwash, an electric razor, opened vitamin pills and dental floss. The other shelves were as cleanly polished as if he had just moved in. Rosa quickly dried her hands on a terrycloth dressing gown. Although she had quit a long time ago, she felt the urge to smoke a cigarette. Back in the living room, she examined the collection of spirits on the bar trolley that stood in the corner next to the sofa: gin with gold flakes. *Traveler* gin from the Seeland region. *Turicum* gin with lime blossom from the Lindenhof. *Ticino* gin from the Valle di Muggio.

'Do you have any red wine?' she called towards the open kitchen.

Later she couldn't remember exactly how it happened. They had circled each other, seemingly by chance. Their voices had grown warmer, their glances across the brimming Chianti glasses more meaningful. As Martin spoke, tracing the story with his hands, Rosa had imagined what his hair would feel like. Or the tender hollow of his collarbone, beneath which his blood pulsed. Her heart must have been beating a hundred and fifty times a minute. Maybe he had taken her hand first. Perhaps she had taken his. Perhaps the backs of their hands had just touched as they simultaneously leant towards the coffee table to flick the ash off their cigarettes. Whichever it had been, the first touch eclipsed everything: the fear of being hurt and the fear of what was to come. She felt his fingertips on her neck. He kissed her slowly. If he had kissed her quickly, the thoughts in Rosa's head would not have become heavy. But as it was, they sank down like sediments did to the bottom of the sea after a storm. She felt his firm muscles as he lifted her up and laid her on the bed. Her skin burnt from his stubble. She dug her fingers into his back and pulled him towards her. He kissed her neck passionately. Lips and hands wandered until everything became touch. Rosa groped her way towards the bedside table—and switched off the light.

14

T HE NEXT MORNING, Rosa didn't know where she was at first. Traffic was roaring past behind the closed shutters. The air was stifling, her eyes were gummed up. Sour breath came out of her half-open mouth. She felt someone's heavy arm on her hip. The memories returned hazily. She turned on to her side, at which the mattress also began to move. Strips of light fell through the chinks and illuminated the room. She looked for something to fix her gaze on. Like the racing bike hanging on the wall. Or the succulents on the shelf next to it. When Martin got up shortly afterwards, she pretended to be asleep; with her eyes closed, the dizziness was almost unbearable. When he had disappeared into the bathroom, she gathered up her clothes. Eventually she found her crumpled knickers, which had slipped into the gap between the two mattresses. Rosa quickly got dressed. A futile attempt to slip back into yesterday's body.

When she got home, Rosa first took a lukewarm bath and scrubbed the night off her skin. Remnants of soap bubbles drifted over the surface of the water like clouds or shifting continents. Then she felt sick. After a while, the only thing that she could vomit out was green bile. Shivering, she knelt in front of the toilet bowl and pressed her forehead down on to the cool tiles. Bathwater dripped off her body and formed small pools on the floor.

The curtains in the nearby houses were still closed. Furry black bees swarmed around blossoms in unchanging circles, and the buzzing of their transparent wings was the loudest thing to be heard. Rosa had divided the kitchen garden into four square beds. The routine that it demanded of her had saved her more than once. She began to pick tomatoes before they shrivelled; wild currant tomatoes that were only marginally larger than the fruit after which they were named. It did her good to witness the countless transformations that took place here. When seeds turned into tender shoots that broke through the soil, when yellow blossoms turned into green tomatoes and the plants found their form with each brightening day. It all happened according to an ancient plan, which could not be disturbed by anything until these deep-red fruits appeared. Not much more was needed. Rosa picked up the misshapen ceramic bowl and started picking stones out of the flower beds so wildly that she flicked soil into her eyes. She leant against the moss-covered wall, exhausted. She pulled the sleeve of her shirt over her hand and wiped away the blur of tears. She could smell the nicotine on her fingers through the fabric and quickly buried her hands in the ground again. Why did people always want more? Why did she herself want more? If she hadn't had the damn urge to have a baby, she wouldn't have broken up with Leo. She would never have gone to a fertility clinic. She certainly wouldn't have gone on a date with Martin Weiss—and she wouldn't have to ask herself now whether they had used condoms from the opened packet last night. Or not.

15

'DO YOU HAVE A MOMENT?' Fred asked—but essentially it wasn't a question her boss was asking. Rosa straightened her shoulders and followed him down the freshly polished corridor to his office. It was next to the command centre and had the best view of the lake. She had just been on her way to the service kitchen in search of a very strong cup of coffee. Had he noticed anything? Beneath the starched shirt of her uniform she was bone-tired, and yet wide awake from the night. The clock above Fred's desk showed half past three. Rosa tried to ignore her growing headache, and watched a boat gliding across the water with full sails.

'How are you actually?' Fred asked. And smiled, which created deep creases round his eyes. *How are you actually?* The question was as simple as it was banal, apart from the *actually*. Rosa thought she could hear concern in the question that went beyond the professional. Fred had been a widower for some years, and although he demanded a lot, he was very perceptive when it came to his employees, even if he tried hard to hide it.

'Quite well, *actually*,' she said. She still felt uncomfortable about their last conversation.

'You've met Andrea Ryser already,' he said. The creases had disappeared. 'I'll keep it short: as you're the only one here at Forellensteig who has had forensic training, we'd like you to reduce your regular shift work in the coming weeks. Instead you will take on a sort of interface role in the Moritz Jansen case.'

Rosa had expected that she would have to comb the lake for clues, take water samples, maybe even attend an extended team meeting. But she certainly didn't expect him to send her back to what she had fled from before she started at Forellensteig. She pressed her hands tightly under her thighs to stop herself from saying the wrong thing. Then she looked up.

'And she knows… about my connection?'

'Of course! But we agreed that the advantages outweigh the disadvantages. Anyway, it's enough if the others know that your sister was undergoing treatment there. What you told me the other day stays between us,' Fred said, and got up with a glance at his watch. 'By the way. The fire squad officer in charge already needs assistance today—you're to meet him in one hour. It's about the establishment that rents out the motor yacht. I think it's called Neaira or something like that. You were first on the scene that morning when the boat was found. Lots of good reasons, right?'

Rosa knew that she wouldn't come up with a quick-witted response—it would take until her bath that evening, or when she was cycling home—so she didn't even try to change

Fred's mind. At least it had one advantage: she could get to her cup of coffee sooner.

Manon put the cappuccino down in front of her. The bistro was one of the few places in town where you could still order chocolate powder on the milk foam without getting a strange look. Rosa put the newspaper aside. On the front page was an article about the demonstration: *Open Science activists storm university*. The flag with the stylized key took up almost the entire page. At the bottom left of the flagpole, Rosa recognized the man with the jewelled facemask who had served her the molecular iced tea.

'You look tired. Wait…' Manon returned with dark chocolate mocha beans wrapped in gold paper. 'They're miracle workers,' she promised.

'I could use them.' Rosa bit down on the bean and cracked it. With a wave of her hand, Manon indicated to one of the waiters to take over at the bar. Then she pulled up a chair and sat down. 'Still the Leo thing?' she asked as she adjusted the collar of her playful petticoat dress, which contrasted with her dyed blonde hair which was growing out and her colourful tattoos.

'I'd almost forgotten about him. Actually.' Rosa trickled a thin layer of granulated sugar on the milk foam until it formed a delicate crust. If it had been mid-morning, she would have dunked a croissant into it or, even better, one of Manon's raisin pastries. But at this time of day, the display case had long been empty.

'Come on, it will be all right,' Manon tried to comfort her, still blaming Rosa's dejection on the break-up with Leo. The two of them had been regulars at her place, so she had witnessed the impending drama from up close. 'When I found out at a routine check-up five years ago that I couldn't have children, it was as if I had been robbed of something that I didn't even know at the time how much I would want one day.' Manon pressed her fingertips into the skin on her breastbone as she spoke. There, a tattooed swallow raised its iridescent blue wings.

'I just don't know what I would regret more later,' Rosa said, and spooned up the last bit of foam from the edge of her cup. 'Either I would always have the feeling that there was a gap in my life that I didn't dare to fill with a family, or I would have to leave the maritime police and start a completely new life.' She took a few deep breaths. 'And then I'm afraid that I only want a child to make me the best possible version of myself.'

'Don't overthink it. The moment will come and then you'll know whether you should let go or hold on.' Manon stroked her tattoo. 'People used to get a swallow tattoo when someone close to them died. For me, it stands for a child that will never exist. And the freedom that that has given me. How would I have been able to take over this wonderful café as a mother of small children?' She allowed her gaze to wander across the room. Over the sky-blue soda siphons and Ricard jugs in which water was served with the pastis. Over the leather-upholstered bistro tables beneath the silver mirrors, where one could observe what was happening at the other tables without being noticed. 'There are two sides to everything. It's all a matter of the optics.' The sound of clinking glasses and slamming fridge drawers from the direction of the bar announced new orders. 'I'll bring you another. It's on the house.' Manon picked up the empty coffee cup and hurried off with light steps.

Rosa was just in the process of studying the new flyer advertising the Café-Med, a regular meeting at Manon's to discuss medical issues, when a shadow fell on her.

'Who would have thought we'd meet again so soon, Zambrano,' Martin rolled the 'r' of Zambrano a bit too long. Otherwise he acted as if nothing had happened. He sat down on the chair opposite.

'I had to rush off to work early today,' Rosa mumbled into her cup, although early could be interpreted generously; her shift hadn't started until noon. The wooden chair creaked as he leant back and pocketed the black Ray-Bans that he had been wearing. Rosa would have loved to find something about him that irritated her, so as to create some distance. She looked at his hands, delicate yet strong; they felt soft, as she now knew. The buzz of voices from Zähringerplatz drifted in through the open windows.

Martin ordered a double espresso and removed his tablet from its cover. 'The last hours before Jansen's death are like a closed book; no messages, no calls,' he said. 'His phone still hasn't been found. It's probably at the bottom of the lake somewhere.'

'Have you received the data analysis from the phone company yet?' Rosa enquired.

'It's always quite expensive. Ryser is hesitating as long as it is considered an unusual death and not a murder. Spending public money, the usual. The only things we can access for now are the mobile data and messages from his computer. At least there is the antenna mast search. Jansen was located for the last time on Friday night at the Chinese Garden around half past eleven. According to Forensics, the time of death was between four and six in the morning.'

'That is strange,' Rosa said pensively. 'I was swimming at the lake that very morning, a bit further down, near the rowing club. Everything seemed so quiet.'

'It was bedlam in the Chinese Garden that night, we can forget about finding any witnesses. But a pedalo hire guy near the mooring slot of the *Venus* made an interesting observation: the motor yacht was out that day, but in the afternoon, around five. He recognized one of the escort women who is there regularly. The description of her companion is Jansen down to a T.' He flipped through his reporter's notebook. 'The woman is called Antonia Schelbert. We haven't been able to reach her yet. Either she has a new phone number or she has done a runner. She already has a criminal record, so we were able to match her fingerprints with those on the *Venus*. Perfect match.'

'And what's on the record?' Rosa asked.

'A few years ago she broke security tags at the Gucci shop on Bahnhofstrasse with a pair of nail scissors and tried to walk out with a backpack full of designer clothes.' Drily he added: 'She finances these in a different way today. By the way, Neaira is just round the corner, opposite the city mission.'

'The infamous corner...' Rosa said. The situation with drunk and violent clients on the former sex workers' patch had got so out of control a few years ago that the residents of the old town had rebelled. No one dared to go into the surrounding shops, which were already struggling to survive. After the protests, parts of the red-light district moved to other neighbourhoods—until eventually there was no more room there either for the visible misery. Now the city government was running an official 'sex drive-in area'. It was located on the outskirts of the city, squeezed between a container village for asylum seekers and cheap artists' studios, and resembled a row of car washes with open 'garage-like cubicles' for cars, and now even for bicycles.

'Do you remember those mysterious deaths a few years ago?' Martin asked. He counted out some coins that exactly matched the price of his espresso and put them on the table. 'Two punters fell out of exactly the same window in a brothel. The investigations went in all directions. But as there was no evidence of suicide or foul play, the whole thing was filed away as an unfortunate coincidence.'

'Let me guess,' Rosa said curiously. 'It's the same brothel that rents the motor yacht?'

'Almost. They're in the same building.'

16

WORLDS COLLIDED in Häringstrasse, even if the short medieval alley began as it ended: with the sex trade. The Dolce Vita nightclub was in the corner building on the old town side and the Love Solarium at the foot of the hill on which the two universities were enthroned. In between, it was typical Niederdorf. Tourists poked into their melted cheese in discarded cable car cabins, even in high summer, with a view of the pewter shop, which only continued to exist because the guilds ordered engraved cups for their parade every year. Business was better in the boutique for bondage gear, which promised its customers 'a strictly good time' with its exquisite leather wrist restraints and latex masks.

The historic location, just five minutes' walk from the main train station, had been perfect for Sophie Laroux's plans when she had bought the top floor of the pale-pink house a few years ago. After several of his punters had died, the previous owner, a former client, had offered her the 'interesting commercial space' at an outrageously good price. In the converted flat with a view of the Alps and the lake, feminism and high heels had since formed a close union. While the sex workers on the lower floors stood behind colourfully lit windows at night like figures in an oversized display case, Laroux was aiming for a different market segment. Her escorts were part of a tradition of clever women, dating back to ancient Greece, who had the courage to lead a free, unattached life. Sophie Laroux sold an upmarket service that was completely in keeping with the spirit of the times: sexual pleasure without emotional entanglements. Although money did also radiate an erotic potency that should not be underestimated and also provided the necessary distance... A melodic gong interrupted the silence in the rooftop flat. Laroux could already hear from the footsteps that the two visitors in the stairwell must be police officers, which she confirmed with a glance at the screen of the camera system that filmed the entrance areas on all four floors of the building. She typed a quick text message and smoothed out the wrinkles on her silk blouse, then opened the door with a radiant smile before the doorbell rang again.

When Martin and Rosa got to the top, a lady in a pencil skirt was already expecting them. Sophie Laroux, whose real name was Susanne Roth, smiled broadly, as is often the way with people who regularly have their teeth bleached.

'*Oh là là.* You got yourself some reinforcements?' she asked Martin, and looked Rosa up and down. 'I thought we had settled everything at our *rencontre* at the station...' With a flirtatious swing of her hips, Laroux turned and led the way. The 'living room' consisted of a Ligne Roset seating area; heavy curtains darkened the room. The spacious rooftop flat was furnished in a mixture of designer furniture and shabby chic, as found in boutique hotels in all the world's metropolises.

'As you can see, I just provide a protected space for meetings here,' said Sophie Laroux. 'The rest is between escort and client—male or female.' She gave Rosa a meaningful look.

'We also have attractive offers by women for women...' Then she flung back the floor-length curtains in a single movement. The sun's rays fell on half a dozen orchids, which were clearly dusted regularly. Apart from that, the room with its dark colours was not made for daylight.

'We are here to serve a summons to Antonia Schelbert,' Martin said firmly.

'You mean Tonya?' Laroux corrected him, as if only the courtesan names that she had made up herself applied in the establishment. 'To what does she owe the honour?'

'We'll tell her when we find her,' Martin replied. 'But perhaps you should have another look in your calendar to see if the *Venus* wasn't booked the day before Moritz Jansen's death after all.' Martin indicated towards an elegant high desk and an open book with handwritten pages. 'Why did you deny that Jansen booked one of your girls on to the yacht on Friday?'

Rosa knew that Martin didn't need to bluff. Alongside the pedalo hirer's testimony, they also had factual evidence—the *Venus* had been covered in Tonya's fingerprints.

With a sigh, Laroux sat down in one of the armchairs that faced each other, as in a therapist's office, with a small table in the middle. 'I wanted to spare Jansen's family. In the case of such a *sudden* and far too *early* death, it is all the more important to preserve the memory.' Her expression was as affected as if she were speaking to a group of mourners and not the police. 'Between us,' she continued, 'it wasn't the first time he behaved conspicuously lately. He was a long-term client, but recently he increasingly turned up in, let's say, a desperate state. Searching for closeness, for something to counteract the emptiness inside...' She went back to the high desk. When she pushed the calendar aside, a button appeared. 'I had this installed for just such situations. My staff from the lower floors would then escort Jansen out on to the street, kindly but firmly. The next day he usually sent a bouquet of long-stemmed roses. Not an isolated case, by the way. We absorb quite a bit of the pressure that is generated in society—you can't possibly imagine.'

A gong sounded and Sophie Laroux excused herself and left the room.

'What is this place anyway?' Rosa asked Martin, and slumped down into one of the armchairs. In addition to her tiredness, she now realized that she hadn't really eaten anything all day.

'Perhaps you could call it a kind of feminist escort service for discerning clients.' Martin went over to the window, which was four floors above the spot where the two punters had hit the pavement. 'I think she thinks she is undermining the patriarchy when she dominates men with sexual charms. Or, to put it better: allows herself to be dominated.' He turned and pointed to a life-size statue of a naked woman with one arm raised as if in battle. 'And along the way she also makes a shitload of money out of it.'

'May I introduce Kilian Graf? My lawyer.'

A man with a beard and a flowing mane of hair followed Sophie Laroux into the room. He was powerfully built and you could easily have taken him for a member of a heavy metal band if he hadn't worn his tailored suit with an indifference that seemed to show with every movement that money became unimportant once you had enough of it. Laroux's introduction wasn't necessary. They both knew Graf. But a second figure emerged from the dimly lit hallway.

'Tonya! Where have you been, darling?' Laroux feigned surprise and brushed her lips against Tonya's forehead.

The woman was discreetly made up; in her modest outfit, she might have passed as a student. Or as a young scientist. But she radiated something else too. Rosa couldn't quite put her finger on it, but she looked as if she was accustomed to using her petite body, in which she clearly felt comfortable, to good effect.

'I only found out about Jansen's death a short while ago…' Tonya said, placing a crumpled piece of paper on the glass table. 'And I thought we could clear up this misunderstanding straight away.'

It was a boarding pass. Martin picked it up and read out: 'Antonia Schelbert, Zurich–Berlin, LX970… Boarding 19.40 p.m.'

If it was genuine, then Tonya had a good alibi for the night for the night of the murder, which is why Martin suggested continuing the interview at the station on Mühleweg, in line with protocol.

'My client would prefer to do the interview right here,' the lawyer said, and opened his briefcase. 'You can record the interview by hand, correct?'

A vein throbbed on Martin's forehead as he recited the rights and obligations so that the statement would have legal validity. For the next fifteen minutes, Tonya spoke in a low but clear voice. She confirmed that she had actually met Jansen that afternoon on the *Venus*. They had drunk champagne and Jansen had seemed stressed. When the moment came where the client was supposed to deposit an open envelope with cash in plain sight, he had not done so. He had then dropped her off at the next harbour and had headed out on to the lake again. When a regular client on a business trip asked for a spontaneous meeting in Berlin shortly afterwards, Tonya had immediately packed her suitcase.

'Why didn't your boss know anything about the meeting with Jansen?' Martin enquired, but was interrupted by the lawyer.

'I would like to point out that neither of my clients are obliged to give any further information in this context.' Graf pulled several sheets of paper from his briefcase. His fingers sported several heavy rings with diamond-encrusted skull and crossbones and coiled snakes. 'This is a written contract between Neaira GmbH and its employees. With this, my client here'—he pointed to Sophie Laroux—'disclaims any liability for what happens after the transaction has been concluded on these premises. This particularly applies to the use of the *Venus*, whereby in any case the motor yacht is hired by the client himself, by the hour or overnight.'

Graf was one of the most colourful lawyers in the country and repeatedly campaigned for the 'self-determination of sex workers' with daring but media-savvy actions. In the process, he set off storms of indignation among women's organizations and incurred the accusation of using the women to enhance his personal reputation.

'You can bring all the documents with you when we question the witness at the station,' Martin said.

'Unfortunately, my schedule is very full,' replied the lawyer.

Martin's eyes flashed, but Rosa gave a signal for them to leave. They wouldn't find out any more here today.

But Martin wasn't prepared to let up yet. 'You can get up to five years for making a false statement in a murder investigation. It would be better if you came up with more information.'

He fixed his gaze on the two women in turn, then slammed his business card down on the open reservation book at the door.

'What was that all about?' Rosa asked as they stepped back out on to the summery street.

'I can't stand that guy.' Martin produced a crooked menthol cigarette with dry tobacco trickling from it.

'I would never have known,' Rosa said. They walked a few steps and were soon back at Chez Manon. There were now bowls of crisps and olives on the tables. 'So what do you think? All these dead punters—is Laroux on a feminist vendetta against the male sex or what?'

'I don't know,' said Martin, 'There are certainly some strange gaps in the stories.' He looked around restlessly.

'Shall we have a drink?' Rosa blurted out.

Martin stepped on the half-smoked cigarette butt. 'No offence, but I wanted to fit in a run up the Uetliberg... I'll see you tomorrow.' And with an absent smile he was gone.

Puzzled, Rosa watched him go, then she pulled out her phone. Three missed calls. Three voice messages. Although otherwise completely different, Stella was just like her mother in this respect. Even after all these years, Rosa had not been able to get them out of the habit of calling several times in a row. In the past, she had called back as soon as possible, always slightly worried, but now it led to the opposite reflex: she set the ringtone to mute.

At home, Rosa cut off a large chunk of butter and took two eggs out of the carton. They lay cool and heavy in her hands before she cracked them on the edge of the pan. The egg whites sizzled and set. Rosa felt as if an age had passed since she'd woken up in Martin's flat that morning, so much had happened since. She couldn't really explain his changeable behaviour. Perhaps he was just a moody person? Or maybe he was uncomfortable with them working together? It hadn't been her idea, but she had to admit that her curiosity was piqued. The circumstances of Jansen's death were very odd indeed. She didn't know how or why, but there had to be more to his death than the rather too obvious arrangement of a party night on the motorboat made it seem.

Rosa yawned heartily with her mouth open, then spread coarse-grained mustard on a piece of brown bread and placed the fried eggs on top. As always, she ate the white of the egg first and then dipped the rest of the bread into the yolk, which tasted warm and comforting.

T HE ACRID SMELL of patchouli and incense wafted
     around Ellie Jansen. Normally, Rosa would have won-
dered how a fully conscious person could occupy so much
olfactory space. But this case was different. Ellie Jansen, a
mother of two, former psychiatric nurse and freelance inte-
rior designer, had just been made a widow, which was not
changed by the ongoing divorce proceedings. Moreover, Rosa
and Martin hadn't announced their visit, but had driven at
short notice to the neighbourhood on the right bank of the
lake, a good twenty minutes from the fertility clinic. The light
bungalow stood out from the neighbouring half-timbered
buildings, which were overgrown with climbing roses. The
back of the garden was protected by hedges and artificial
mounds according to Far Eastern principles. They entered
the house via a terrace shaded by the roof. If Rosa hadn't
known it to be the same person, she would never have connected this woman with the picture on Jansen's desk. She
had a beautiful face that was bloated from medication. The
flowing dress with its puffed sleeves could not distract from
her bony arms. Her hands hung down as if her extremities
had lost all their strength.

'Are you moving?' Rosa pointed to the dining table, which could easily seat ten people, with stacks of household goods on it, and the Eames chairs that had been pushed together. The living room looked as if someone had picked up every single object in it and then forgotten to put it back. Magazines were spilling out of an open sideboard, sofa cushions were scattered on the floor and a hand-woven kilim was rolled up beneath the high window. The harmony of the lily pond in the garden, spanned by a Japanese-style bridge, pointed up the chaos inside the house.

'The energy in the room is not flowing properly any more.' Ellie Jansen reached for a basket, from which a huge monstera was growing, and placed it on the side table.

'We were unable to reach you on the phone...' Martin began.

She paused for a moment, then she continued to pluck at the dark-green, slotted leaves and mumbled: 'As if the house had been placed on a water vein overnight.'

'Mrs Jansen?'

Her hands shook. 'At first I had the feeling he wanted to punish me. But it should have been the other way round.'

She leant her back against the wall and suddenly slumped down to the ground.

'I'll fetch a glass of water,' Martin said, and disappeared in the direction of the spacious kitchen.

'You would actually think,' said Ellie Jansen, without looking at Rosa, who had hurried over, 'that it wouldn't be so bad if someone dies and you had already separated from them, and their things aren't there any more. You'd think it's not as bad as if his chair is suddenly empty, his clothes still hanging in the cupboard. But that is not true.'

Without a word, Rosa sat down next to her on the stone tiles, which were pleasantly warm.

'The empty chair could be filled at some point. The cupboard emptied, the things given away,' the widow continued. 'But there is nothing here any more. At least nothing that meant anything to him.'

Martin returned and handed Ellie Jansen a glass of water which she accepted with a nod. In the same moment, hoarse voices approached from outside. They wavered between too high and too low, as if they had accidentally escaped from their owners. Shortly afterwards, two teenagers appeared in the doorway. Despite the heat, they were wearing black Supreme hoodies. Their faces, blooming with acne, looked completely unprotected, as if they still lacked the defence mechanisms of adults who had learnt to hide their feelings. They both pulled their caps down until their faces were hidden. Rosa felt caught in her thoughts.

Ellie Jansen had already straightened up. She walked towards them with a straight back, her expression brightening with each step. Even without their air-cushioned trainers, the twins would have towered over their mother by a good head.

'Tim! Karl! Look, this is…' She turned back to Rosa and Martin, who then introduced themselves, but the two boys, who had thrown their black backpacks into a corner, wanted one thing above all: to get out as quickly as possible. They ignored the plate of biscuits and the glasses of milk their mother had put out for them, instead asking for money 'for something proper'.

'They blame me,' said Ellie Jansen after the twins had disappeared, on their way to a kebab shop in the harbour. She propped her arms on the shiny wood-clad kitchen island. 'I get it.' She dug out a pack of Marlboro Red from the drawer and switched on the extractor fan. 'Daddy's girl, that's what my mother used to call me. Would you like one?'

Rosa made a dismissive movement. 'I gave up years ago.' She thought of her own father, whose woollen jacket had always carried the smell of wood smoke and shaving cream. How he held a too-short pencil in his dinner-plate-sized hand, which was more suited to chopping down trees than correcting schoolchildren's dictation. Even though her parents still shared a flat in the old town, at least officially, there had always been two sides to her family. Her side and his side. And the more her mother rejected Vinzenz, the more Rosa took his side. Even though he had never asked her to.

'Is there a law that says that children always side with the one who leaves them? No matter what the person did before that?' the widow asked.

'Perhaps that's the only possible way from their perspective, because they only notice what is missing,' Rosa said, handing her the ashtray from the window sill. Below it, on the sideboard, some apples and bananas shrivelled in a bowl, around which buzzed a handsome collection of fruit flies. Rosa had to smile when she noticed that someone had placed carnivorous plants in a clay pot painted with skulls and crossbows alongside.

'I don't know why I am telling you all this. I am actually paying an armada of therapists.' Ellie Jansen laughed drily. 'Moritz was obsessed with his work. And addicted to women. Always new women. The assistants in the surgery got younger and younger. He could deny it as much as he liked, I'm sure that he cheated on me again and again. And that another woman was behind the split. You can tell these things.' The memory of past humiliations seemed to boost her.

Martin took advantage of the resulting pause to ask Ellie Jansen for her particulars and to inform her of her rights and duties in the interview. Rosa had understood, even without his silent request: she would take the minutes.

'Forgive my direct question,' Martin said, 'but do you happen to know whether your husband ever used the services of an escort agency?'

'Not that I know of, but it would fit.'

Ellie Jansen's index finger twitched slightly as she brought the cigarette to her mouth. 'Why?' She exhaled a cloud of smoke as she asked the question.

'Does the establishment Neaira mean anything to you?'

'Nothing at all.' She stubbed out the half-smoked cigarette and clenched her hands into fists, hiding them under her upper arms.

'Were drugs an issue?' Martin continued.

The widow frowned, which might have been hiding a wish for an explanation, like someone with an unknown ailment hopes for a diagnosis that would at least end the uncertainty.

'The Moritz that I knew hated to lose control. His mother was a pill popper. He had an almost hypochondriacal fear that he had inherited a sort of addiction gene from her. He was obsessed with the topic ever since he got involved with the start-up…'

'Addiction?'

'No, genetic inheritance. He was hoping for a big breakthrough.'

'Just so we're talking about the same thing,' Rosa interrupted, 'you mean a special area of the fertility clinic?'

'No. That was basically running itself… CRISPR-Cure is the name of the company. An acquaintance of his from his student days founded it. The laboratory is in an office complex in Zug. I've only been there once.' She raised her eyebrows, furrowing her forehead in the process. 'It's not my world. He didn't talk about it much. Not even while we were discussing the issue of maintenance. That was the last time I saw him.'

A ringtone grew increasingly loud. 'Excuse me, I have to get that,' Martin said to the widow and thanked her for her time.

'I'll come to the car later,' Rosa called out as he left the room. Then she sat down on one of the bar stools next to the sideboard and asked Ellie Jansen when that had been.

'About three weeks ago. He actually thought he could just fob me and the children off financially. He couldn't get away with that with me though! I had settlement proceedings instituted in court. He didn't even feel the need to respond to the summons. That was one of his deceitful games.'

When she too left shortly afterwards, Rosa pointed to the flesh-eating fruit fly trap. 'They're clever, your boys. Eventually they're bound to recognize it—what's there.'

18

M ARTIN WAS SITTING on some low steps by the har-
bourfront. He hadn't noticed her yet. Rosa stopped
for a moment and enjoyed the scenery. She was magically
attracted to harbours, even if small ones. And this one here,
like many other things in this Alpine country, definitely
deserved a diminutive. And yet everything that made a
proper harbour was here. There was constant coming and
going. There were boats with names like *Mona Lisa* and
Victor, and cygnets preened their grey plumage. There were
captains with navy-blue caps; and surfers, even if the waves
they rode came from a motorboat. Martin held up his phone
triumphantly when he spotted Rosa:

'Star lawyer or not… Antonia Schelbert, sorry, Tonya,
wants to make a statement after all. Alone.'

They walked over to the shade of the trees where the
Jaguar, which must have dated back from the early nine-
ties, was parked. Martin's work car was in for a service, so
they had used his private car for the trip to the lake town,
even though his boss would not have approved. He leant
across the empty passenger seat and opened the car door
from the inside. Before she got in Rosa took off her blazer,

which had been hiding her gun belt. She was sweating. She would upload the report of Ellie Jansen's questioning that evening. In this respect, the criminal police were no different to the maritime or local police: no evidence without a written report. Even the clearest confessions were not valid if they weren't recorded in writing. Every day there was a meeting where all the departments involved in the case came together. Martin would later be applying for a search warrant for the start-up premises.

'Can you drop me off at Forellensteig on the way?' Rosa asked.

Martin nodded and switched on the car radio. As they drove off, Rosa saw the twins sitting in the Seeperle, their hoods pulled right over their heads.

Picturesque hills with vines passed by on the right, criss-crossed by footpaths. The world's largest area of cultivation for *Räuschling* was by Lake Zurich. But the old grape variety was hardly cultivated any more. The road followed the shore, past banks overgrown with brambles and a disused factory site where discarded freight wagons were rusting away. When the church with its late-Gothic tower appeared Martin turned off the road, but the car ferry had just left. They took up position at the head of one of the marked lanes that reached up to the railing hung with geranium boxes on the landing stage. Martin turned off the ignition, and the inside of the car was quiet. *I really hope he doesn't want to talk about the day before yesterday,* Rosa thought.

As if he had only just remembered, Martin said: 'We should have found the documents on the start-up when we searched the fertility clinic, given how well maintained the book-keeping and patient database were.'

'Maybe he has another office? A second server?' The response didn't really convince Rosa either. You couldn't even buy a parking ticket without identifying yourself in this country. How could Jansen have made his stake in an entire company disappear?' 'He might have been a silent partner... what was the story about a mistress? Wasn't there any evidence of a woman in the studio above the surgery?'

'Maybe his ex just wanted to blacken his name.' Martin watched the swallows sailing around the church tower. He cleared his throat and said: 'If all is fair in love and war, then a disputed divorce must be a hell made up of them both.'

'Do you think that the widow had anything to do with his death?' Rosa asked doubtfully.

'I could imagine that she wanted to end the conflict,' Martin said. 'To free herself from a burden... and I am sure she is deeply hurt. But on the night in question she was at a health cure in Wildhaus, we checked her alibi.'

Martin started the engine as the next ferry arrived in the harbour. The barrier was raised and the convoy started moving. The bicycles were allowed on the ramp first, followed by the rest. A red-faced man directed them to a parking space on deck, waving a fluorescent lamp in a slightly stressed manner. Martin put the car into gear and pulled the handbrake. The nodding Elvis on the dashboard of the car began to vibrate like everything else on the ship did when its engines started.

Although the crossing only took ten minutes, it was ten minutes of freedom every time, because whether it was Corfu, Sardinia or Horgen, the procedures were the same, although the ferries in this area were almost regarded as floating bridges. From the glove compartment Martin pulled out a punched card that was probably as old as the car itself.

'Is this still valid?' he asked and held the card out to the red-faced man. The man, in turn, beamed as if he had met an acquaintance he hadn't seen for a long time. 'Naturally, unlimited, that's what it says.' He whipped out a ticket punch to mark the trip.

They got out of the car and walked over to the railing. Rosa's hair fluttered in the wind as she looked out over the lake. Square window panes were set into the high sides of the ferry; the frames were painted the same blue as the domes on the Greek island of Santorini. They framed the landscape behind them, the bushy shorelines, the houses with balconies over which beach towels hung, the lake that grew increasingly narrow towards the city and the semicircular overlapping chains of hills which in the hazy light looked like they had been painted by a child. Rosa blinked over at Martin. *He's not thinking that I want something from him? Or is he? Why doesn't he say anything?* She could taste blood on her tongue. Without realizing it, she had bitten off some dry skin on her bottom lip. She was looking for a tissue when Martin started to speak. 'I don't want to offend you or anything.'

Rosa paused in surprise and pressed the tissue to her lip.

'But there is another woman in my life, another story, a difficult story.' He had very much enjoyed being with Rosa, Martin continued, but he did not feel ready 'for more', even if the night had been very nice. 'I think it's better if we only see each other at work for now,' he concluded.

'I was going to say the same to you,' Rosa said a little too quickly, because she could hardly bear the awkward look on his face. 'I have just gone through a break-up too—and I want to do my own thing for the time being.' *He had enjoyed it? It had been nice?* The repetition felt to Rosa like charity she hadn't asked for.

She stared at the blue-framed window pane which turned the world behind it into a picture. Perhaps a little too monotonous, always the same route, always the same image, but at least it was clearly defined. And she wished she could put together the slivers of memory from that night too. But she was filled with restlessness, bright and lively, like the spray on the waves.

The bleached planks leading to the entrance of the pavilion on Forellensteig had never felt so good under her feet as on this early evening after she had got out of Martin's car with a brief goodbye. The *Venus* was still anchored in the hangar, which was also home to the maritime control authority; it was distinguished from the other pleasure boats and yachts only by the luminous tape on the tarpaulin.

'Rosa!' The smell of fried onions, the mother of all cooking smells, came from the service kitchen. Karim had tied an apron over his uniform. 'Are you going to eat with us?'

Unlike their colleagues in town, the maritime police didn't have a canteen. They took turns cooking for the team.

'You can't imagine how happy I am to do that!' Rosa sat down on the corner bench beneath a long glass façade.

'Are you making progress?' There was a hiss as Karim put strips of peppers and fennel into the shallow frying pan.

'A little, it's complicated. Martin is applying for a search warrant at the public prosecutor's office for a company in Zug that Jansen was involved with. Something to do with genetic engineering. But quite honestly, I'd rather work the night shift here. By the way, how is Georgina?'

'She's already gone. But a male is still swimming around, guarding the clutch of eggs.' He added bay leaves, turmeric and cayenne pepper to the round grains of rice and deglazed them with stock ladled from a steaming saucepan.

Fred came into the room. 'You're here, Rosa? Great! Then we can talk right away.'

She walked wistfully past the kitchen counter, where Karim was now sprinkling saffron threads into the vegetable paella. Instantly, the inimitable smell of sea air, of sweet, dried hay and rusty metal wafted around. She took a deep breath and followed Fred into the meeting room, where he projected a map of the lake on to the wall. The places where they had taken samples were marked in yellow. One of them was not far from the fertility clinic.

'We sent everything to the lab,' Fred said. Then he opened the monthly schedule to go over Rosa's shifts at Forellensteig and reduce them to a minimum. She still secretly hoped he wouldn't be able to fill the schedule without her. Even in normal times, they were quite short-staffed. This was down to the budget, as well as the fact that the maritime police officers could not simply be replaced by colleagues from the normal force. For the work on the lake, in addition to a diving licence, you also needed a sailing licence and various other advanced training courses. But Fred didn't bat an eyelid as he redistributed the shifts and handed her the printed documents from the lab. A few minutes later, the ship's bell sounded from the gallery: dinner was ready.

9

T HE SUN SHONE through a milky sky. Outside the
    Neumarkttheater, loading ramps with crates of drinks
whirred up and down, barrows heavily loaded with sacks
rumbled across the cobblestones. A carpet of noise that was
as much a part of the morning here as the piercing bells
of the four large churches in the old town. Water dripped
from Rosa's hair, evaporating almost as soon as it ran down
her back. The early morning swim in the lake had slightly
calmed the conflicting feelings that she had had after hear-
ing from Alba.

> While everything outside calmly carries on as usual, we marvel at how
> delicately this life is woven. Especially where it touches the threshold to
> infinity. Ancient knowledge is written all over your face; and you have
> a serenity that is only found in the very old or the very young.
>
> Welcome to our world, Marin Alexander!
>
> Katrin & Alba
>
> Overjoyed.

Rosa was relieved that the birth seemed to have gone well.
Originally, Katrin and Alba had planned to get pregnant at

the same time. That way they would not only have shared the physical changes, but also everything that came later. But at some point they abandoned the plan. Rosa didn't know why and didn't ask when Katrin's pregnancy worked out.

Rosa filled two bottles with spring water at the Nike fountain and put them in the seagrass basket that always reminded her of the market in the South of France where she had bought it. Then she filled a third bottle and drank in hearty gulps. The seats in front of the theatre café still lay in the shade of the row of houses, which did not detract from their popularity. Time seemed to have stood still in Neumarktgasse, which led from Seilergraben down to Niederdorf, as a glance at the historical model in the architectural archives would have confirmed. Instead of mass-produced goods from international chain shops, here you could buy fine wool and handmade soap, and in the guild house where Lenin once planned the revolution progressive performances were now being rehearsed in a theatre. Josefa was sitting with her wire-haired dachshund Anselmo next to a folded sunshade on the edge of the village boulevard. Instead of the usual carafe of white wine 'to thin the blood' that she treated herself to after her morning walk, today champagne was fizzing in a flute glass.

'What a festive day!' She happily raised her glass towards Rosa and ran her hand through her henna-red hair. Her eyes, rimmed with black eyeliner, and her entire face glowed as if a light had been switched on inside her. 'Let's drink to Marin Alexander, my youngest grandson!'

Rosa couldn't remember Josefa being this excited about her other two grandchildren.

'All right,' she replied. 'But just an espresso for me.'

Anselmo sniffed Rosa's trousers with interest. She wondered what it would be like if she could also sniff out who the person she was with had met up with. *Better not*, she thought as she glanced over towards her mother. Josefa was known everywhere in Niederdorf. Sometimes in the past there was no getting through the crowd when she played the accordion on a chair outside the Spanish bodega; the instrument propped up on her long legs, she knew how to create an intimacy that drew everyone in, much to her three daughters' chagrin. Now Josefa lit a *beedi*. She could have woken the dead with the Indian cigarette made from rolled tendu leaf—it was very dry and very strongly perfumed. Rosa had initially hoped that it was another of her mother's temporary fads. She had almost forgotten most of them already—Josefa's enthusiasm for tap dancing, her calligraphy phase… Josefa wanted to drive out to the old farmhouse where Alba lived to visit the new parents and the baby. Rosa, on the other hand, didn't want to impose so soon after the birth, but she was going to give her mother something to take along. There was only one way of congratulating someone in Rosa's book—with a homemade pot of soup.

Pablo's grocery store looked just like you would want a toy shop to look as a child. Grapes with dark leaves rested beneath a blue and white striped awning. Fragrant Decana pears, their stems sealed with red wax. Fist-sized Amalfi lemons. Small, crisp apples and velvety dates. The day's specials were chalked up on slate boards. *Smoked salmon. Freshly made sandwiches. Lemon ravioli.* Inside, syrup bottles and liqueurs glowed like liquid amber. Behind the glass panes of a buzzing refrigerated counter you could find smoked mozzarella, wild boar ham and pickled anchovy fillets. The shop had simply always been there for as long as Rosa could remember, like the sky between the rows of medieval houses, like the rustling leaves of the ash tree in autumn or her sisters' impatient footsteps on the sloping steps in the stairwell. Perhaps the shop was the reason why she always wandered through the supermarket aisles first when she was abroad. It was only when the words and the writing on the packaging jumped out at her in a different language that she really felt like she was somewhere else. She would select the most beautifully packaged products for her shopping basket: bars of chocolate with long-forgotten cartoon characters on them, *La belle-iloise* sardine tins depicting lighthouses and fishing boats, each tin a still life, although once open they smelt just as bad as they were good to look at.

Pablo also had Art Deco biscuit tins and tubs of sea salt flakes with shaded mermaids whose bare breasts were surrounded by clouds of hair. But today Rosa limited herself to the ingredients for her soup. After a brief chat, she paid as people queued up behind her.

R ICHI BENT DOWN to pick up a wet sock that had slipped off the washing line. Then he reattached it next to the other clothes, which, judging by their fit and size, were not all his. Although they lived less than twenty metres away from each other, Rosa hadn't seen him since her dinner in the Black Garden. He was clearly avoiding her. Or he was so busy with Erik that he no longer had time for her? Had he got into this relationship a bit too quickly?

It was probably better to steer the conversation on to neutral ground first. And indeed, Richi did loosen up a bit when he was telling her about the new Dürrenmatt production at the theatre. He was playing the role of the physicist Möbius, who has discovered nothing less than the 'world formula' and has himself locked up in a mental institution so that his research results don't fall into the wrong hands.

'The end is a bit predictable,' said Richi. 'Friedrich Dürrenmatt wrote: the more human beings proceed by plan, the more effectively they may be hit by accident, and it must *always* lead to the worst possible turn of events, at least on stage. That's why Möbius burns his manuscript at the end of the play for the benefit of mankind.'

'Would that also mean,' Rosa asked, 'that people who meticulously plan a crime are much more vulnerable than those who act on impulse?' She sighed. 'In the case I am working on, we could do with a bit of dramatic coincidence.'

Over time, Rosa had developed a form of communicating with Richi that allowed her to talk about work without giving away official secrets, or at least almost. While they gathered snails from the vegetable patches, she told Richi about the start-up in Zug that had only existed for five years but was already earning tens of millions of dollars a year. Well-known pharmaceutical companies were among the investors, and research was being carried out on a commercial method by which DNA could be specifically altered.

'In principle, that would mean the biological elimination of chance. I am struggling to understand it,' Rosa concluded.

'I'm afraid I can't be much help there either,' said Richi, and sat down on the ivy-covered wall that bordered the gardens of the houses of the Stüssihofstatt. 'But why don't you speak to Erik? He knows about that sort of thing.'

Rosa would have liked to tell him that sometimes it was enough for him to just listen to her, play back what she told him, made her aware of inconsistencies. But she realized that it was important for Richi that she should develop an independent relationship with his new partner. So she nodded as she ran her fingers over the heavy head of a faded artichoke. Tubular flowers burst like purple fireworks from the thorny leaves. Each year Rosa left one or two specimens because she could never decide whether artichokes were better eaten or simply admired. 'Do you really think he has time for that?' She reached for the plastic sandpit bucket and the soup spoon again. A snail was trying to climb up the handle. Rosa couldn't bring herself to pour boiling water over them, which is why the little creatures were collected every morning and released in a nearby park.

'Of course. If you want, you can go and see him at the university clinic later.' Richi tucked his phone back into the back pocket of his jeans.

'Perhaps I can fit it in before the meeting.' Rosa plucked indecisively at the green of a carrot. 'Yes, perhaps that would be a good idea.'

With a jerk, she pulled one of the French touchon carrots out of the ground, bright red-orange and *sans coeur*. Since she wanted to make the soup straight away, Rosa put a sieve on the snail bucket she had filled with torn-off greens and weighed it all down with a stone.

'Tell me…' Rosa scraped dried earth off her fingernails. 'Is everything OK between us?'

'Actually, I would have thought that you would have let me in on the egg-freezing thing. But it works for you, then it works for me.' He held out his open hands to her and added: 'But the subject of babies is not off the cards, at least not for me.'

His embrace and the crook between his neck and shoulder where Rosa rested her head felt as familiar as the sound that came from her kitchen a little later.

In the Spanish village where her Yaya had grown up, every birth also meant a death. Not only the one that was contained in every new life anyway, which was inevitably heading for an end: at every birth, the boniest, toughest chicken made its way into the cooking pot. A circle that closed with death, when family and friends spent days saying goodbye to the laid-out body, and bubbling away on the stove was a soup that was constantly replenished with stock, chopped vegetables and fresh tears. Rosa's grandmother had taken this tradition with her when she and her husband, both very young and only married a few weeks, went to the South of France to work—and stayed. No one knew exactly how many beginnings and endings had been witnessed by the soup pot that Rosa had inherited after her grandmother, over ninety years old, passed away on a bone-chilling cold New Year's night.

Rosa put the pot on the stove. On this hot day, the coconut oil had melted into a transparent liquid. She rubbed some of it into the dry ends of her hair before putting enough into the pot to cover the copper bottom. Then she pressed the gas ignition button several times in quick succession because you never knew when it would click. Alba and Katrin lived on the outskirts of the city, together with two dozen animals that they had saved from the slaughterhouse. So chicken soup was out of the question. Instead Rosa had come up with a recipe with shiitake mushrooms, dates and star anise for the new mothers. If Richi kept an eye on the simmering soup, then she could actually stop by Erik's before her meeting with the prosecutor.

*

'In short, CRISPR/Cas is in some ways the most important hope of modern medicine.'

Erik and Rosa were sitting on one the university clinic's leafy terraces with cups of vending-machine coffee in their hands.

'And yet the research is prohibited?' Rosa pulled out a second chair and put her legs, heavy from the heat, on it.

'Not necessarily,' Erik replied. 'But red lines have been drawn as to how far research is allowed to go. And the biggest red line is interfering with the human germline, because everything that is done to the genome is passed on to future generations.' An air ambulance approached noisily. Erik continued in a louder voice. 'It's not yet clear whether manipulated genomes become unstable after one or two generations. That is probably the biggest danger.'

They watched in silence as the helicopter landed on the roof of the next-door building. It was so close that they could feel the downdraught of the whirring rotor blades. Within a few seconds the stretcher, surrounded by people, had disappeared between the automatic doors. Seconds like a narrow gangplank between two eternities from which the seriously injured person threatened to fall.

'In some people,' Erik continued, 'the blood cells deform into sickles and they suffer terrible pain. Many never reach adulthood. The culprit is a single mutation from a single point in their genome. Sickle cell disease is supposed to be the first to be cured by genetic scissors.'

Over the next fifteen minutes he explained to Rosa why the dream of gene therapy was controversial. The first experiments had been carried out more than fifty years ago. Most of them failed, sometimes with dramatic consequences for those being treated. In the case of sickle cell disease, researchers were accused of using African-American people as guinea pigs, since they are affected more often than other ethnic groups. The researchers, as well as the companies who held the patent, did not mention the severe side effects. Despite all criticism, the hope for a future cure for Alzheimer's, cancer or Parkinson's disease remained. Rosa thought she recalled that CRISPR-Cure also had a therapy for sickle cell anaemia in its portfolio. Just the thought of it made her feel uncomfortable.

'You see, it's high stakes.' Erik turned the bottom of the paper cup in his hand. 'But these are faced by unimaginable numbers. If the research is successful, it could mean a cure for hundreds of millions of people who are also suffering from a monogenetic disease. Ultimately, politics will decide. Societal debate, or simply necessity.'

He downed the last of his coffee and placed the empty cup on the stone slabs.

'Perhaps it's just a few years too early for our society?' Rosa asked.

'When I think about what I see here every day'—he indicated towards the blue awnings of the hospital—'I don't think so.'

'I know that it is hard for a lot of people to get involved with things they can't control and don't understand,' Rosa continued. 'Especially when they are not affected themselves.'

As she said that, she realized that she had never given the subject much thought either. Because everyone in her family was healthy, a fortunate chance. Now Rosa felt a little ashamed of how much she had always taken it for granted.

'That is probably right,' Erik said with a frown. 'But maybe we also have to have more respect for the unique era we are living in. When misery and suffering are no longer the result of predetermined fate but of society's sensitivities, then something is very wrong in this society.'

ROSA LOCKED UP HER BIKE. On the art college campus opposite, students were walking down the curved ramp. It used to serve as an access road to the dairy, the largest of its kind in all of Europe at the time. After this closed, the striking building housed a legendary techno club for a while, high up on the seventh floor, which presented a different image of Zurich to the world from the idyllic postcard city with its Alpine panorama. Rosa's younger sister, Alba, had thrown herself wholeheartedly into the nightlife, which often ran on into the next day and sometimes into the following night too. For a long time leading up to this point the sisters had had a difficult relationship, covertly controlled by their mother. Depending on your point of view, Alba was perhaps also fighting for something that Rosa had always taken for granted: her father's recognition. The fronts within the family had hardened more and more until they could only be broken with a huge rupture. In retrospect, it had probably been a liberation for Alba to dive into a temporary world of sound and dazzling excess, in which she not only learnt to say no but also to love herself (and women). Despite the many worries that Rosa had

had at the time, she had to admit that the two of them had been closer since then. Aside from the grey concrete access ramp to the art college, nothing else recalled this epoch of Zurich nightlife. Rosa was amazed at how easy it seemed to be to structurally overwrite places. Since space was scarce in the city centre, the various police crime departments had been centralized a few years ago in a new building here on Mühleweg—in the midst of the party mile in the former industrial quarter.

While Rosa waited for the prosecutor, she inspected the pre-printed flipchart sheets that were attached to the wall with magnets with the instructions from the past week: *Question social circle. Identify social circle. Identify witnesses. Psychological reports. Evidence analysis. Findings analysis. Data carrier analysis. Crime reconstruction.* Since Rosa only had a liaison role in the case, she was—in contrast to the prosecutor, who kept tabs on all of it—lacking the overall picture, even if Martin tried to keep her informed. The consensus in the investigation team was that someone was trying to disguise the doctor's death as an accident while he was under the influence of drugs. At least from Rosa's point of view as a patient, Jansen had seemed to be the type of person who had things under control. But perhaps someone who was driven to excel in his career needed to compensate elsewhere. In the red-light district there were entire fetish scenes that were geared towards providing that kind of compensation.

At least they now knew that Tonya had indeed got on the plane that evening to meet her regular client in Berlin. The airline had confirmed it. But if she hadn't been on the boat that night with Jansen, who had? Martin had homed in on Neaira, but Rosa wasn't so sure: Martin's dislike of the lawyer, who had previously made one or two investigations difficult for him, didn't help the situation. That afternoon, he was going with a colleague to interview Tonya. Maybe that would shed some light on the matter.

'Rosa Zambrano from the maritime police,' Ryser said delightedly and closed the glass door to the hallway. 'I am curious to see the lab results.'

She directed Rosa to a chair at the circular meeting table that filled the back half of her office. Then she poured two glasses of mineral water.

'Our people have been hard at work despite us being extremely busy now that it's summer,' said Rosa, and pointed to a map of the lake. She explained all the places where the blue-green algae were found and which methods had been used to take samples in which areas to narrow down the crime scene.

'Do cyanobacteria even have DNA?' Ryser asked.

'They do. It's a bit like trees where the DNA of a single leaf matches that of the tree it comes from.' Rosa had asked a colleague in the lab to confirm this again, just to be on the safe side.

'So in theory, it would be possible to assign the blue-green algae DNA from Jansen's lungs to the algal carpet from which it originated?' Ryser asked.

'In theory, yes. In practice, however, it would be difficult. You'd have to do a comprehensive comparative analysis that also takes into account mutations and contamination.'

Rosa imagined she could see the numbers whirring behind Ryser's smooth forehead.

'Then let's have the sediments we found and the composition of the plankton at the five sites examined again—that seems to make more sense to me. Especially in the shore zone by the fertility clinic,' the prosecutor said. 'Otherwise we simply have several possible crime scenes.'

'Jansen's widow has hinted that he had extramarital affairs,' Rosa said as she packed her bag. 'Did you find anything out about that?'

'We found very few personal items in the studio above the surgery. But there is a number he was in touch with a lot over the last few months. Guess who it belongs to?'

Rosa shrugged her shoulders. 'His mistress?'

'She is registered as Donald Duck from Duckburg.'

'Really? Do people still do that?'

'Unfortunately all the time. In Langstrasse there's a kiosk on almost every corner that sells SIM cards without checking for ID.'

Rosa was about to get up when Ryser cleared her throat.

'Can I ask you a personal question?' The prosecutor's usually slightly tense features softened a bit.

Rosa sat back down.

'Have you checked what happened to the results of your egg-freezing?'

'I haven't thought about that at all,' Rosa said, trying not to show how shocked she was.

'I thought of it earlier,' the prosecutor said in a professional tone once more. 'Our colleagues only looked at the electronic patient files from the computer, but it certainly wouldn't hurt to compare them with the physical files in the practice. Do you want to take care of that after the search in Zug on Monday? I can get a patrol to unlock the door for you.'

The conversation was still going around in her head that afternoon when she handed her mother the soup for the new parents. Josefa loaded the cardboard box containing the hot glass bottles, padded out with scrunched-up newspapers, into the back of her three-wheeled Velosolex, which was parked in front of the entrance of the cabinetmaker's. She adored this French monstrosity, the unsuccessful marriage of bicycle and moped, with faded fabric roses on the handlebars—even if it was in for repair more often than she herself went to the hairdresser. Anselmo sniffed at the bottles while Josefa chatted with her daughter in her own unique way.

Outsiders wouldn't have noticed anything, but Rosa could hear the more or less elegantly framed reproach in every sentence.

'And you *really* don't want to come along?'

Conversations with Josefa sometimes felt like phone calls where you hear feedback from your own voice.

'No. I *really* don't.'

'Tell me, do you have a problem with the fact…' Josefa began.

'With the fact that I am the oldest and don't have any children of my own? Is *that* what you are trying to say?' Rosa spoke more loudly than she meant to. She quickly looked up at the façade of the building to see if the windows to Richi's flat were closed. She was in luck.

Her mother sighed theatrically and put Anselmo in the dog box that was bolted to the floor of the luggage carrier.

Shortly afterwards, the two of them disappeared in a cloud of exhaust fumes. On the way back to the house, Rosa pulled out a silver pocketknife. She didn't know what was wrong with her. Perhaps it was because she could have been expecting a baby at the same time as her nephew was born—if only Leo had shared her wish.

She tore herself away from the thought and cut a lettuce from the outside in, leaving the heart. Then she picked some herbs. Mint, basil, lovage. Just as she was about to mix a light vinaigrette of red wine vinegar, olive oil and wild fermented radishes for dinner, her phone lit up. *Tonya didn't really come out with it,* wrote Martin, who had just finished the interview at *Mühleweg. I think she is frightened. We need to keep a close eye on her.* Rosa wondered what they had missed.

And then she called her father.

22

T HE BELLS OF THE Fraumünster church were ringing out five o'clock when Rosa turned in on the path to Paradeplatz. Vinzenz had spontaneously suggested a walk in the old botanical garden. Her father didn't often contact her, but she knew that he would drop everything if she really needed him. A newlywed couple were posing on the Münsterbrücke. Grains of rice on the tarmac marked the way back to the nearby Stadthaus, where the registry office was. The bride was wearing a wreath of flowers on her loose, windswept hair. Seagulls screeched in the air. Rosa got off her bicycle and weaved her way through the crowd of guests. The city centre around the Lindenhofhügel on the other side of the river could only be reached by bridges. When she was a child, Vinzenz sometimes brought her maps from school. Rosa never tired of tracing the outline of the island that was formed by the Limmat, the lake, the Sihl and the Schanzengraben canal with her finger. And when she turned the map slightly to the left and looked at it long enough, the island turned into a sitting raven with the Platzspitz, the tongue of land at the confluence of the Sihl and Limmat, as its beak. Rosa had to smile when she thought of it. Then she got back on her bicycle and soon reached the canal at Schanzengraben, which had a rather Venetian ambience with its curved walkways and lanterns.

'That bad?' asked Vinzenz, who had been waiting for his eldest daughter on a bench next to the tropical greenhouse.

'Worse,' said Rosa.

He hugged her briefly but firmly. 'You know what she's like…'

'And someone who is like that can get away with anything?'

'She doesn't mean any harm.'

'Why do you always defend her? You too would rather be in your little hut in the woods than with her.'

'OK, you win. You mother is a terrible person who only thinks of herself. Happy now?' he asked, not entirely seriously, although Rosa felt he had a point. But admittedly, her mother did have a few good sides to her too.

'Have you been to see Alba and the baby yet?' Rosa changed the subject.

'Maybe next week…' he said grudgingly.

Rosa wouldn't have expected any other response. Vinzenz indicated down towards the canal, where canoeists armed with paddles were chasing a white ball and throwing it towards the goals stretched across the water. They watched for a while, knowing that they didn't need to speak in order to feel close to one another.

Later they had a sweet and sour soup on the canal bank. Leaves from the robinias and willows, whose branches hung down as far as the covered rowing boats in some places, drifted on the moss-green surface of the water. A few mallards were dabbling with their tail feathers in the air as the rising noise from the street heralded the approaching weekend.

'How is work going?' Vinzenz asked, lowering his spoon. 'Josefa told me you are with the crime squad now?'

'She's exaggerating. I am just helping out with an investigation, a homicide. Unfortunately, the dead man was also my doctor.' Rosa outlined how she had sought treatment with Jansen on Alba's recommendation.

'Now I completely understand why you suddenly broke up with Leo. I liked him.'

'I'm sorry, but Leo really doesn't matter any more,' she said, and leant forwards. 'Back to the case. I sometimes think that almost all crimes are the result of an imbalance: when the characteristics, traumas, desires that every person carries within them come into a disastrous relationship with the outside world, then they can unleash a catastrophic potential and have a destructive effect.'

'I have had the same thought,' Vinzenz said. 'It is shocking how little it takes to kill someone. In principle, just the uncontrollable urge to cross this line, and the readiness to resort to violence.'

'Exactly,' said Rosa, breaking the wooden chopsticks apart to fish the glass noodles out of the bowl. 'That's why I don't think that all the evidence, forensics and proof to which everyone in the police attaches so much importance are that important. We need to find out how these unfathomable forces came about. The answer must be somewhere in the network that the doctor was at the centre of.'

It was already getting dark when they said their goodbyes. Rosa watched her father as he walked towards the station with long strides and was soon swallowed up by the groups of people on the pavement.

23

IN THE HALF-LIGHT, the railway viaduct looked like a man-made mountain massif. Rosa emerged from the market hall at its eastern end. It was very early on Monday morning, and she had taken the opportunity to stroll among the stalls and buy a few *pains au chocolat* before the morning briefing. The nearby playground was still gapingly empty; just one clearly involuntarily sleepless father making lonely rounds with a pram. Indignant yelling drifted across. Above them, a train rattled towards the main station. Rosa walked past the grove of black pines whose branches cast jagged shadows on the ground.

She had studied the files again until deep into the night. Forensics had searched the motor yacht for specks of paint, for the finest fabric particles and, of course, for DNA. It had been teeming with the latter; there must have been quite a bit going on in the days before. Jansen had also left numerous traces, but nothing suggested a concrete course of events. The toxicology report that had been prepared in addition to the autopsy had been somewhat more conclusive. The substances found in Jansen's blood matched those found on the yacht after an initial rough analysis. But that didn't necessarily mean anything. Rosa thought of the Lucerne

'Nurse of Death' who had killed twenty-two elderly people, all of them patients. The biggest serial murder case in Swiss history had remained undiscovered for a long, shockingly long time, because the nurse killed where death was lurking round every corner anyway—in intensive care. In Jansen's case, too, they had no proof that it was murder.

Martin was waiting outside the entrance, his hands buried in his pockets, the sound of the motorway bridge and the reduced glow of the night lights behind him. He held a plastic card to the sensor, the door opened, and he let her go in first. Rosa felt his gaze on her back.

'Stairs or lift?' Martin asked, already energetically climbing the first few steps.

Rosa followed him to the first landing, then she stopped and rummaged in her backpack for the empty water bottle. 'I am just going to fill this up…' she explained.

She entered the toilets, lit up in pale blue, which smelt of lemon and toilet block, went into one of the cubicles and locked the door behind her. Still no blood. Nothing. Just grey scratchy toilet paper. Still, it was highly unlikely that anything had happened. All the eggs from her previous cycle were stored in a tank of liquid nitrogen. And maybe they had used a condom?

Martin was waiting by the stairs. 'Another few minutes…?' he said. Rosa realized that she was still holding the empty water bottle in her hand.

'Blast!' she said, and turned on her heel.

*

CID, the department that dealt exclusively with homicides or grievous bodily harm, was on the top floor. Rosa put the paper bakery bag on the table in the investigation team's office and tore the paper sideways, so that the crispy puff pastry appeared. Then she took a seat at the far corner, as there seemed to be no fixed seating arrangement. There was no one there yet apart from her and Martin and the minute-taker anyway.

As if on cue, this changed. The bag rustled joyfully every time the experts from the other departments arrived. The delegation from the neighbouring canton where the start-up was located would meet them on site.

'This is top of the priority list,' Andrea Ryser said, and impatiently tapped on the white board, which showed the area of the upcoming search, with her felt pen. Next to it was a large map of Lake Zurich. The place where the body had been found was marked with a number; the five blue-green algae carpets were also marked, as were possible routes the yacht might have taken that night.

Ryser pointed to a family photo of Jansen. 'The deceased was in the middle of divorce proceedings and his lawyer said that the wife was playing hardball.'

It was the photograph that Rosa knew from Jansen's desk, but now it appeared in a different light. The storybook family. The sunset. The sea. Now that Rosa knew how the family had broken up, she felt pity as well as irritation.

Next to it, Ryser pinned a letter with the city's official letterhead. 'We found a summons from the divorce court in the dead man's studio. Clearly he didn't feel like arguing. The letter had not been opened.' She looked around insistently. 'A gynaecologist pumped full of drugs, a mysterious accident, a high-class prostitute and an angry ex-wife. We are not just searching a company today, we are looking for a murder motive. And perhaps for a mistress.'

24

T HE SKY ABOVE the motorway seemed to grow a little wider all the time, at least that's how it seemed to Rosa. Perhaps because most of the time the motorway went through flat countryside, where uniform fields with mono-culture crops, treetops, sometimes a farm, a few scattered fruit trees passed by the side windows. Perhaps because the motorway was not just a road but always also a possibility. Even if the journey, like the one to Lake Zug now, barely lasted more than half an hour. Rosa imagined just continu-ing to drive. To follow the signposts towards the Gotthard Tunnel, to the south side of the Alps, to the next sea, perhaps the port of Genoa, perhaps Marseilles or the Venice lagoon. Where there were hotel rooms with sea views, brass beds and crocheted bedspreads.

Martin was concentrating on the road. Among the camper vans loaded with mountain bikes and the lorries they could also see the dark cars of their colleagues who would accom-pany them on the mission. There was quite a lot of traffic that morning. Martin had to keep slamming on the brakes. He didn't swear, at least not loudly, that wouldn't have suited him. But the knuckles of his hands on the wheel were white, and he was driving unnecessarily aggressively. Rosa felt relief that she was no longer seeing anyone. No moods. No communication minefields. Instead of half-heartedly engaging Martin in conversation, she started reading up online for the upcoming search.

The crypto valley between Baar and Zug had become world-famous over the last few years, an El Dorado for the digital finance industry that offered legal security, business-friendly tax incentives and parameters and 'reduced regulations'. Conditions that not only attracted crypto gold prospectors, but all kinds of companies looking for a secretive environment. So alongside commodities trading, shell company business was also flourishing in this small, very small brother of Silicon Valley. Rosa had no doubt that a start-up which, according to newspaper reports, was working on using 'genetic scissors to penetrate the deepest human structure and eradicate errors there' would feel right at home in this place.

Rosa's sister Valentina had also lived in Zug ever since she married Oliver. He was a commodities trader, and there was always tension because he and Rosa were not on the same wavelength politically. Their house was on a hill overlooking Lake Zug and provided enough space for the children, as Valentina kept pointing out as if she had to justify the fact that, for her husband's sake, she had moved out of the old town. Something that Rosa would never do. Not for anything in the world.

CRISPR-Cure was located at the end of a street that was home to two dozen companies, just a stone's throw away from

Zug railway station. Their plain façades showed little of the digital and medical revolutions going on behind them. It had also started to drizzle; a thick blanket of clouds hung in the sky. And yet, with a bit of imagination, the dead-straight road could have been in Palo Alto. As in San Francisco Bay, young people sat in Starbucks early in the morning in the glow of their open laptops in front of Americanos and tall vanilla lattes. Snatches of English drifted over in passing, giving a sense of a collaborative spirit. CRISPR-Cure occupied two floors in the building complex where a Swedish company took care of the virtual transactions of its high-net-worth clients, as Martin noticed with a sideways glance at the two Bentleys with waiting chauffeurs. In the lobby, Rosa sat down in one of the designer chairs with chrome steel feet and discreetly watched the goings-on from there. Since most of the relevant data was stored on the start-up's internal servers, the IT specialists from the team were on first. At the same time, two external scientific experts would inspect the lab, with appropriate respect, of course. On a flat screen on the wall of the lobby, a CRISPR-Cure promotional film was running on an endless loop, the style of which reminded Rosa of a TED talk or a tech conference, where company bosses prophetically presented their latest products on almost bare stages. Animated graphics explained the principle of the genetic scissors—disrupt, delete, correct or insert—while their use was explained by researchers in white coats during a tracking shot through the in-house lab. A particular image that appeared caught Rosa's attention. She was able to pull out her phone just in time to take a picture of the screen. It showed two middle-aged women in pastel-coloured cocktail dresses. They were standing on some sort of red carpet; behind them was an advertising wall showing the logo of a well-known pharmaceutical company. They stood with their legs artistically posed like models. With her fingertips, Rosa enlarged the image on her phone. Now she knew why the name of the company's founder had sounded so familiar: there was no doubt. She was looking at the beaming face of the immaculately dressed woman who had given a speech at Genetic Science Days.

'Ravi Kathoon, Chief Commercial Officer,' she heard a voice say in an English accent, introducing himself with a touch of irritation that was not uncommon in these situations. Kathoon asked Rosa and Martin to follow him to the cafeteria for a chat. Cafeteria was taking it a bit far—there was a self-service bar, a couple of plastic indoor palm trees and two angular sofas that didn't look as if anyone was ever able to relax on them. There were more flatscreens on the wall showing Google Earth images, which seemed to be as much a part of the corporate culture here as Post-its and energy drinks. They sat down at the first of the six tables. Martin explained to the manager the events that had made this search necessary. When Kathoon heard of Jansen's death, his expression froze. He blinked several times as if he needed to refocus his gaze, then produced an e-cigarette, which emitted the tangy scent of vanilla, reminding Rosa of the air freshener in Stella's car.

After a few puffs, Kathoon regained his voice: 'We at CRISPR-Cure will, of course, do everything in our power to assist you in the investigation.' He stood up and offered them something to drink, making Rosa think he needed a reason to move around more than anything else. They declined. The water dispenser bubbled as he filled a plastic cup for himself.

'Then why don't you explain Moritz Jansen's role within the company?' Rosa said, switching on the recording device.

'He is a developer in the company, together with Marie Duval.' Kathoon explained how the company had gathered enormous momentum in the last three years since Jansen joined. It was considered an insider tip at the stock exchange where it was soon to be listed. Those who knew about the company mentioned CRISPR-Cure in the same breath as the likes of Tesla and Spotify.

'Look at this landscape,' he said, indicating the red-sand plateaus of the Grand Canyon on the screen on the wall. 'These rivers have carved deep canyons. You can read a billion years of Earth's history from their walls.'

Kathoon ran the tip of his e-cigarette over the layers of rock shaped by the water. 'Imagine, only three centimetres of this canyon came about in the entire history of mankind.' He paused briefly, as if he had given this speech several times before and knew exactly at which point to pause to increase the tension. 'The history of science could be compressed into one millimetre. And since we started studying genes, maybe a tenth of a micrometre has passed. In terms of

Earth's history, we are no more than the blink of an eye. But if we were able to'—he turned back to the canyon and traced the canyon down to its base—'take all this… into our own hands? What if this one blink of an eye were enough to control the processes that had previously been subject to millions of years of evolution?'

'That would end in disaster. In an ethical catastrophe,' the historian in Rosa said spontaneously.

'Maybe. But it could also be the case that CRISPR technology is where humanity has been heading for since its origins.' He switched off the screen. 'If we don't try, we'll never find out.'

When Rosa left the start-up, rain was still drumming on the leaves of the trees along the street. She breathed a sigh of relief and walked the short distance to the station. Martin and his other colleagues would be busy for several more hours.

Kathoon hadn't exactly seemed overcome by grief. She had the feeling that he put the company above all else. Perhaps not the company in the strict sense, but the purpose it pursued. It wasn't about the money—or at least not just that—but more about the kind of power that can't be bought, almost God-like, a power over life and death. When she arrived at the station, Rosa typed a message to Andrea Ryser, telling her that she would arrive at the surgery around quarter past two. Rosa hoped that she had interpreted the 'assignment' properly, namely as indirect support to check her own medical records.

With a last glance towards the Zugerberg, Rosa boarded the train and resolved to drop in on Valentina soon. Valentina complained—quite rightly—that Rosa never visited her. It was primarily because of her irregular work schedule, but that was not the only reason.

On the train, Rosa sat down in an empty compartment. Shortly after Horgen, the sky opened up; seagulls circled over the water, which broke in gentle waves on the shore. She would have liked to take a photograph, but she knew it wasn't possible to capture what she saw. Instead she pulled up the photo of Duval on the red carpet once again. *Are we allowed to do everything we are able to do?* Duval had asked in her speech at Genetic Science Days. Rosa was sure that the skilful researcher would answer in favour of this. In the course of history, again and again people had believed that their supposedly higher goals also gave them the authority to break the law or to reshape it in their favour. Regardless of anyone they hurt in the process.

25

THE FERTILITY CLINIC seemed unreal, like a forgotten backdrop after the end of filming. The ornamental fountain in the reception area had dried up, and the Buddha looked pale without the cleverly arranged lighting. Only the aquarium that rested on a glass stand glowed purplish-blue in the waiting room. Rosa looked around for fish food on the lacquered sideboards on which piles of magazines such as *Geo*, *National Geographic* and *Mare* were laid out, but then she realized that an aquarium of this size would have an automatic feeding system. It was actually discreetly tucked away just above the water level. Rosa paused for a few minutes and observed the colourful underwater world. Then she took out her pad and made a note that someone should come by and service the system. A door with coffered windows led from the waiting room directly into the garden. Rays of sunlight now broke through the cloud cover, heavenly spotlight that shone directly on to the bronze-red foliage of a majestic copper beech. Rosa unlocked the door and stepped outside. Heavy drops clung to the red tips of the leaves, which seemed to turn greener when you stood directly below them. She went down to the shore. The villa which housed the fertility clinic had direct access not only to the lake, but also to a whitewashed boathouse surrounded by waving reeds. A jetty led out on to the water. Moored to a pole in the water was a dinghy like the ones used to get to sailing boats that were anchored on buoys further out. Rosa pulled the small boat closer; as she did so, another rope appeared at the stern. She reached for it and was about to throw it back into the water when she noticed the knot. It was not tied with an ordinary loop, but with a constrictor knot. You didn't see those very often, although it was one of the strongest knots there were. Since her time with the Girl Guides, Rosa had had an obsession with knots, which she later followed up as a historian. Knots were older than almost anything else that had been handed down in human history. For cave dwellers, a loop had been the best method to catch food. Later, the first pile dwellings were held together with knotted tendons and ropes. Rosa was convinced that the inventors of the first knots should be classified on the same level as those who had found out how to make fire, use the wind, make a wheel and till the earth. In shipping, a simple bowline was usually used to tie boats to a bollard or to a mother ship. She looked out at the buoys where larger sailboats were moored, wondering what Jansen needed the dinghy for. He had a boathouse, after all.

The heavy door handle opened effortlessly. Light fell on the water, which shimmered jade-green in the inner basin. A vintage speedboat rocked on the gentle waves, polished mahogany, manufacturer Boesch, a popular classic on the lake. Long-dried swimming costumes hung in the changing room. Apparently, Jansen had been a boss who knew that his employees performed better if they could share some of his luxuries.

The chime of her phone announced a new voice message. In quick sentences, Martin explained that the computer analysis had shown a connection between CRISPR-Cure and the Neaira escort service. Rosa was puzzled—a business connection? One that went beyond Moritz Jansen's private pleasure? That would put things in a different light.

Rosa was startled when she saw the time. She quickly typed a message to her colleague Tom at Forellensteig, asking him to check whether another boat was registered to the doctor. Then she hurried back to the surgery and went in search of her patient file, which had to be in the fireproof steel cabinet. One of the uniformed officers handed her the key and then retreated back to the entrance area. She got down on her knees, pulled open the bottom drawer with the letter Z and searched for her surname. When she found the file, she took out her phone and photographed the pages inside. It was only when she was already back at the entrance that Rosa realized she had not got hold of her own patient file, but Alba's. Annoyed, she turned back to find her own file, before leaving the practice together with the police officer. She gratefully accepted the offer of a ride into town. On the way to the patrol car, Rosa took off her latex gloves and stuffed them into her pocket. She wondered whether Martin's suspicions of Neaira hadn't been wrong after all.

26

THE FULLY AUTOMATIC DOORS of the sienna-red cable car closed with a jerk. Inside, students surged between the retro wooden benches, careful not to spill their takeaway coffee or the flask of tea they had brewed in their flat share. The journey from Central to the Swiss Federal Institute of Technology at the top of the hill only took a few minutes, yet the Polybahn was still a city landmark. On the open platform right at the front, a popular insider tip in travel guides, a woman was leaning against the rail. Marie Duval wore a pristine white trouser suit similar in style to those worn by a certain former federal councillor whenever she had to get a delicate deal through Parliament or had to communicate unpleasant decisions at a press conference. Mariel's lecture would start in twenty minutes. The dark circles under her eyes had disappeared under her make-up. After the search at CRISPR-Cure, she and her managing director had talked through all the options until late into the night. They would go ahead as planned with the IPO, but the patent would have to wait for now—until they were no longer the focus of the police investigation. She stretched her tense shoulders. Either way, it would be a sensation.

She thought of the Nobel Prize that a rival laboratory had received a few years ago. Often it was only a matter of weeks. The ruthless system that drove itself ever faster was known as scooping. It had happened to Duval more than once. Years of work were wasted because someone else published first: research funds, recognition, prizes—the winner takes it all.

Her entire life had had just this one goal: to put an end to random repetition. To learn to control those tiny but all the more significant changes that arose from the constant repetition of the same processes and had so far left the course of evolution to chance.

Wasn't that the way all great inventions came about? At the right time, with the right conditions, someone went to the limit of what was possible, sometimes even beyond. If something turned out to be unimportant or not useful, it had to be destroyed again because in the end the only thing that mattered was to recognize something really great when it was in front of you. She had done that. She had even, without hesitation, taken the necessary steps to protect it.

As they approached the upper terminus, silkie hens clucking in the grounds of the care home tried to outdo the sparrows cheeping in the dense hedge. Marie Duval positioned herself in front of the barrier so that she could be the first to get out at the Belle Époque shelter with its overhanging gable roof. She looked back down the rails and for a brief moment, barely more than a breath, she felt as if Moritz were standing next to her on the platform. It had happened to her several times over the last few days. If someone had the same sort of walk. If someone stood out in the crowd wearing the same combination of trousers and light shirt that he always wore in summer, as if he were about to set off on a trip to a tropical country. And yet they had only gone to the Grand Hotel on Lake Brienz, where they kissed behind the waterfall, while tiny frissons cooled her skin. She pushed the memories aside. There was a saying: give someone power and you will discover their true nature. That's how it was. Moritz couldn't handle it. Too soft. Too unstable. Too easily manipulated.

As always when Marie Duval walked past the front of the main building, she was annoyed by the scientific gallery of saints that adorned the façade. Aristotle. Isaac Newton. Conrad Gessner. Leonardo da Vinci. Alexander von Humboldt. James Watt. There would have been a whole series of women who, in their time, also deserved the laurel wreaths despite having the greatest difficulty in obtaining text books. One of the first women to attend university in the seventeenth century had had to sit in a box with peepholes and air vents during lectures, as if to punish her for seeking education. Two centuries later, women were still researching in secret, at kitchen tables, under the cover of their homes. Agnes Pockels, barely twenty years old, built her first apparatus to measure the surface tension of water using her grandfather's discarded chemist's scales and a tin of meat extract. She had

154

got the idea from greasy washing-up water. An American chemist later developed her apparatus a little further. And received the Nobel Prize for it.

Marie Duval thought of the hard drive with the results of her studies, which was safely stored in a locker in the mountain fortress. A shudder passed through her body. It would not happen to her.

S IMON FISLER cut ash-grey skin into even squares until he had divided up the whole back. Then he lifted the squares and folded them to the side. The new students would be arriving in an hour. As their first encounter with death was usually easier for them when they were working with an elderly person, he had selected a seventy-year-old woman with heart failure. The atmosphere here in the pathology basement was challenging enough as it was, and the pungent sweet smell of the formalin used to preserve the corpses would linger in their nostrils for a long time afterwards, despite the very modern ventilation system. The ribs appeared beneath the skin, beneath them a yellow-brown/dark-red tangle. He would reveal the structure of the body layer by layer. Once Fisler had finished his preparations, he threw away his gloves and washed his hands. The analysis of the samples from the dead doctor found in the lake was still pending. The autopsy had been completed, but shortly before the body was to be released for burial Fisler had started to wonder. Something about the dosage of the toxicological substances in the blood was not right. He had taken another sample from the stomach and ordered a comprehensive toxicological screening from the lab. He could then compare the concentration of drugs in the stomach with those in the bloodstream. The more complex screening could—unlike conventional testing methods—detect unusual substances such as ketamine and would hopefully provide information about how the drugs had been administered. His mailbox was full when he started up the computer in the basement's anteroom.

Shortly afterwards, Fisler hurried back into the autopsy room. Moritz Jansen had indeed died from the ketamine, but there was not the slightest trace of it in his stomach. That could only mean one thing.

The pathologist looked at the woman laid out in front of him. It was still a human being. 'I am sorry, there is a change of plan,' he said to her. Then he searched for the correct corpse number. Now the students would start with a drowned body. At least they would get it over with.

28

THE ASH TREE wiped the gleaming sky with broad branches above the skylight. Every night Rosa dreamt, and every morning she could remember what she had dreamt. But in the minutes between waking and getting up the dreams moved further away, lost their contours, just as the shore loses its contours the further away a ship moves from dry land. Until only a pale feeling remained. It was not yet six o'clock. Rosa tried to go back to sleep, but she couldn't. A familiar pulling sensation announced the onset of cramps. All at once she was wide awake.

Relieved, she washed down a painkiller with water straight from the tap. Then she went back to bed. She crumpled up the blanket and curled up on her side. It was only now that she felt free of the unpleasant feeling that had clung to her since that night. And all the more since the annoying conversation on the ferry. She most certainly didn't want to show any weakness in front of Martin. If he didn't recognize her, see who she was, then he wasn't worth it. Now at least she knew what she didn't want. 'And that's a start at least,' Rosa said out loud to herself. Then she picked up the novel that was lying open on her bedside table. The story was set in the kitchen of a Mexican estate. Tita de la Garza is not allowed to marry because she has to take care of her mother. She has no choice but to pour her love into the food she prepares for her disappointed groom Pedro, who has to marry her sister instead. When she cries into the icing of the sugar-white wedding cake, all the guests also end up crying. When Tita crushes chillies with almonds and sesame seeds on the grindstone and beads of sweat make their way through the gap between her breasts, lust also flares up in Pedro's eyes. Fancy Christmas cake. Fried pastries. Every single dish has a consequence. Rosa firmly believed that, even if the effect was not as intense as depicted in the fiction of magic realism, a dish could suggest a feeling or a certain mood because it was a snapshot of a constantly changing world. The seasons were reflected in the food—and with them the whole impact of new life and the passing of time.

After breakfast, Rosa moved to the deckchair under the ash tree with the book, a pot of tea on a stool next to her. Tita catches six quails in the courtyard with her bare hands for a recipe with rose petals. She struggles with killing them. She twists the first quail's neck. But instead of dying, it laments its fate bitterly—with a broken neck. Tita realizes that you can't be squeamish about killing. Either you do it emphatically, or you inflict horrible suffering. Tita's mother, on the other hand, kills as you should: with a blow and without pity.

Rosa put the book down and watched the billowing ash leaves, the fleeing shadow. Perhaps this was the female way of killing. Not aggressively, not emotionally, not through physical superiority. But very calculated, very subtle. And with cold determination.

How ironic would it be if the gynaecologist had been killed by a woman? But they needed evidence or witnesses, or even better both. As long as they didn't have those, they had to accept the statements made by the female suspects. Ryser had extended the focus of the investigation to Marie Duval. The widow was still under surveillance, but she had an alibi for the night of the crime, as did Tonya from the escort agency. Had Jansen been killed out of unrequited love? Or for business interests? Or perhaps both? Or something completely different? Rosa stifled a yawn; she didn't have to be at the university until noon today.

Ryser had called it 'field research'. And so, before Marie Duval was interrogated, Rosa would have the pleasure of attending her first lecture in years.

Rosa pulled another carrot out of the ground. The carrots had done well, because unlike the strawberries, which had a fixed place in the beds all year round, this vegetable made room for something different after a season. Back in the kitchen, Rosa scrubbed the carrots with a vegetable brush, grated them, squeezed lemon over them and put the bowl aside. Many people thought that baking was an exact science that didn't forgive the slightest carelessness. But Rosa managed without a recipe and achieved delicious results thanks to a simple basic calculation: three eggs, cane sugar, butter or vegetable oil, lots of grated nuts and some flour with baking soda. Apart from that, she experimented like a poet plays with words. Today, in addition to the carrots, she added grated walnuts, buttery and full of flavour. Also orange flower water and a dash of Cointreau, although cherry brandy would also have been good.

Shortly afterwards, Rosa put the cake tin into the oven. Then she looked for her tablet and skimmed through the preliminary summary report of the search in Zug. Alongside the main server, CRISPR-Cure had a second system called Human Nature. As parts of it were specially secured, the analysis would take a while longer. But the IT guys had been able to pull up the internally recorded phone calls of the last few months. Here she could see what Martin had referred to in his message yesterday: CRISPR-Cure was not only in regular contact with Jansen's fertility clinic, but also with the noble establishment in Niederdorf. Rosa wondered if Jansen's visits to Neaira might have been a cover for something else. Or whether he had made his private calls through the company number. Sophie Laroux, at least, seemed to be quite enterprising. Might she have another string to her bow besides the agency? A shrill sound startled Rosa. She lifted the cake out on to a sheet to cool down. When she came home later, she would cover it with a paste of mascarpone and icing sugar and drink a very strong mocha with it.

Before she left the house, Rosa took another quick look at her emails. Her face lit up when she read that the number of 'Donald Duck' had been traced in the Bündnerland mountains. This was the number that Jansen had been in frequent contact with in the weeks and months before his death. Rosa's suspicions become more and more urgent. Moritz Jansen, with Marie Duval, his wife and Tonya, had a bewildering number of women around him, but something was still missing. Something that had placed two people in a fatal relationship with each other.

29

'WHICH OF YOU would like to have children?' Arms shooting up showed that Marie Duval's question was not merely rhetorical. Rosa reflexively glanced at Martin's hands, which remained still on the desk in front of him. Of course he didn't respond, why would he? But she had hoped to get some sort of indication from his reaction. A twitch, a clearing of the throat or a shift in position would have sufficed. But he just sat there, motionless and yet tense down to the last fibre of his body. Rosa wondered where this suppressed restlessness came from. They were sitting in the back row of the lecture hall, which was so full that some students had to sit on the steps. There was no doubt about it—when this popular guest professor gave a lecture, it was an event. In the past half-hour, she had spoken about how genome-editing had been a worldwide triumph, revolutionizing genetic engineering and micro medicine. A development that gave science almost infinite power. And with power comes responsibility, as we all know.

'If you raised your hand and you are a woman,' Duval said, 'then you should freeze your eggs. If you are a man, you should think about freezing your sperm. Sooner rather than later.

Regardless of how fertile you are. Regardless of how young you are. Regardless of how healthy you are.' The uncertainty was written all over the students' faces as Duval continued: 'It is pretty certain that the conception of your future child will take place not in the bedroom but in a laboratory, because the current distribution of our genes is nothing but a lottery. A lottery that is perceived as a magical, fateful process. But barely has the child been born than a never-ending battle begins. Against time. Against disease. Against the elements.'

A young woman on the steps spoke up, her hair plaited in a fishtail braid. 'If I understand you correctly, you want to make us understand that it would be best if we genetically manipulated our children. Would you do the same with your children?'

Marie Duval paused for a moment before she replied. 'Good question! It was only seventy years ago that we found out that DNA, the manual of life, is shaped like a twisted rope ladder. Today the code of life is something we can read, write and above all, hack.' Duval walked up and down the podium as if she needed to give her thoughts space as they took shape. 'I would do everything to protect the lives of my children. To keep them safe. To safeguard them from illness and suffering, from human cruelty. And to give them what they need to survive in a world full of competition and struggle.'

The student nodded. 'Then probably the only question left is who even wants to live and have children in a world like that?'

*

Three hours later, in the interview room at police headquarters, Marie Duval's white trouser suit was still not creased in the slightest. 'I live alone with my cats,' she said, and crossed her legs.

'So *no one* can confirm that you were in Kilchberg on the night of Jansen's death?' Martin asked once more.

Rosa pictured the professor coming home in the evenings and Siamese cats, whose fur was as light as her trouser suit, slinking around her legs. She almost felt like tipping the half-full coffee cup across the table, just to see if she was as resistant to stains as she was to Martin's questions.

Duval swiped nonchalantly across the screen of her phone as if she were looking for an appointment in a full calendar and not being interrogated in a suspected murder enquiry.

'Samples don't keep office hours. I was working until half past nine in the evening in the lab in Zug,' Duval said, leaning back in the upholstered chair.

On the way home she had bought some freshwater sushi to take away from the campsite in Wollishofen, then she had read some scientific papers and gone to bed early. 'After all, I had to be fit for the Ironpeople the next morning. I took part together with a friend.'

'When and in which category?' Martin asked.

'Charity category in the sprint triathlon, we were raising money for the children's hospital, and we started at exactly five minutes past eight.' She added, not without pride: 'We didn't need much more than an hour for the distance.'

Martin abruptly changed the subject. 'Your company says that it commercially promotes technologies with which the human genome can be specifically modified and exchanged. Can you explain that to me?'

Rosa knew that Martin was well acquainted with the topic by now and that Duval had probably explained it a thousand times. Not only in the newspaper interviews in the bulging folder in Martin's office. He probably just wanted to hear her explain it. Often it was the barely perceptible timbres in a voice that framed a statement and could provide valuable clues. Less the *what* than the *how*. It also gave them the opportunity to study the professor's facial expressions and gestures again. Sometimes it helped to have a suspect repeat the same thing so many times that they became entangled in contradictions. It might be a long evening. Rosa checked her phone and saw that Tom had sent her a message. No other ship was registered under Jansen's name. Rosa wondered once more why there was a dinghy at the surgery's jetty. Then she concentrated on the interrogation again.

'In principle, it's quite simple,' Duval was saying. 'We are *actually* aiming to cure diseases, not just treat the symptoms. To do this, we exchange faulty sequences and insert the copy of a healthy gene. This then produces many more healthy genes. Sickle cell anaemia, for example, can already be cured using our drugs.'

'Isn't that very controversial because of the side effects?' asked Rosa, who still remembered Erik's explanation.

'If the gene ends up in the wrong place and the wrong

166

sequences are duplicated there, then it can cause cancer. But very soon we will be able to eliminate these unwanted effects. We are standing at the foot of a gigantic mountain. And every drug has side effects,' Duval said. 'You have to judge it by its benefits.'

Martin got up and walked up and down the room. 'How did you know Moritz Jansen?' he asked.

'We completed our doctorates together.'

'Where?'

'In Heidelberg.'

'Were you a couple then?'

'Not really. Even if his wife didn't want to believe it. Moritz was above reproach professionally, at least he used to be. However, in his private life it seemed to that something had broken out lately that he had suppressed during all those years of building up the clinic.'

'So you were close?'

'We were a good team, yes. Of course we occasionally had private chats. Moritz was very open and told me quite a bit, about his marriage, about his affairs. But in the end, the conversation always returned to work.'

'Why was your company in contact with an upmarket escort service in Niederdorf?'

'That's interesting—was it?' Duval put her phone away. 'That must have something to do with Moritz. Lately, he had been mixing things that didn't belong together.'

'Did the two of you have different opinions on the proposed IPO?'

'On the contrary. The prospect of more liquidity suited him very well. You probably know that he was in the middle of a costly divorce… particularly in view of the fact that his new girlfriend was not easy to please.'

'Do you mean Antonia Schelbert?'

'That name doesn't ring a bell.'

'Then perhaps Tonya? No? She used that name too. She works for the escort agency and met Jansen the day before his death.'

Marie Duval snorted. 'Really? Well, well, well. No, with Alina—that was different.'

Rosa exchanged a glance with Martin. Was that the missing link they had been looking for?

'Even if you might think that the story is far too trite—an older man, a young girl. He had completely lost his head,' Duval continued.

'What is the woman's name? How long had they been seeing each other?' Martin asked.

'Alina Orlov. She is a former student of mine. Very talented. Very ambitious. Very ideological. She was already active in the Open Science Movement back then, but then she was kicked out of the university because she hacked into the internal computer. She stole access data to international databases and downloaded paid studies from them and put them online. After her expulsion, she started putting on performances, which were completely unscientific and sensational. As if a social discourse about the future of medicine could be conjured up with illuminated hemp plants, transparent frogs and all the other cheap laboratory tricks. She regularly appeared at conferences and trade fairs. That is where they met.'

'Martin, do you have a moment?' asked Andrea Ryser, who had popped her head round the door. He got up and the two of them talked quietly and then pulled the door shut behind them.

Martin returned a short while later with a stack of papers. 'When were you going to tell us that you had made Moritz Jansen an offer to buy his shares in the company?'

He held a document in front of Duval's face. It must have appeared during the evaluation of the encrypted system of CRISPR-Cure. So Jansen's business partner wanted him out of the company. That certainly changed the situation.

When Martin handed the contract to Rosa, she saw that the signature boxes had not been filled.

'Why hasn't he signed it?' she asked Duval.

'He hadn't signed it *yet*. There is a difference. We already had a date for the signing.'

'Maybe he wanted better conditions?' Martin said. 'Then his death would have come in handy. Suddenly the issue has resolved itself. And you are the main shareholder again. Provided that his heirs were prepared to be bought out.'

'Believe me, a sale would have been the best thing for all concerned...' Duval did not allow herself to be thrown. 'Since Moritz started going out with Alina, he had made several blunders. The relationship, the divorce, his new... lifestyle. It all got too much for him. I think he actually sometimes went to work high. There were also irregularities in his expense accounts. At least with the sale he could have saved face.' As she spoke, Duval knotted her fingers under the table. 'I also know that he passed on internal information to Alina. We can't have someone doing that. The industry doesn't forgive such things.'

'Can you prove your accusations?'

'You will find out about them soon enough, I am quite sure.'

The trams were already pulling into the depot when Rosa finally got on her bicycle and set off home. The street lights were reflected in the pockmarked face of the dark Limmat. *Alina is like the inkblot on the Rorschach test. If she chooses, she can make people see in her exactly what it is that they most desire.* Marie Duval clearly had little sympathy for her former student. She made it sound as if their meeting had been the fateful moment in Moritz Jansen's life that had dragged him into the abyss.

Rosa swerved round a group of teenagers riding electric scooters. She thought of the twins. Of what it must be like not knowing who had killed their father. And pedalled harder.

30

T HE CITY HAD ITS OWN TIDES. Those who lived in it began to follow them at some point. While some of them jumped straight into the shopping crowds on Bahnhofstrasse and the late-night hurly-burly in the former red-light district around Langstrasse, others eschewed it and did something completely different. Rosa was part of the latter group. She was of the opinion that you sometimes had to earn the beauty of the city. By getting up early, for example. She also knew exactly when she had to be at the river to get a spot in the shade. The wooden Art Nouveau baths moored in the Limmat had turrets with curved roofs and, as the oldest of their kind, were reserved for women. Rosa ordered a freshly squeezed orange juice and headed off to find a spot. After Marie Duval's interrogation yesterday, she had been back on normal duties at Forellensteig. A feeling of calm had returned together with the familiar operations. The swans came swimming up the river in a long column at this early hour of the morning. They would spend the rest of the day dabbling in the lake. Cynics claimed that the swans were also a symbol of Zurich—radiant, white and clean from afar, proud and aloof up close. If you wanted to escape the horrendous charges for rents, coffee, buses even—indeed, for all the things you needed every day—and, if nothing else, the legendary gold vaults under the Paradeplatz for a moment, then you headed for the public baths. That too was Zurich. Swimming belonged to the city, which in relation to its population had the highest density of baths in the world, just like its blue trams. The lake and river swimming baths were a microcosm that functioned according to its own rules. On the sunbathing lawns and bleached wooden planks, it didn't matter whether you were born here or moved here, how much money you had in your bank account at the end of the month or whom you loved. There was no better spot on a hot day for eavesdropping on life behind closed eyes as it spread out on your left and right like colourful towels. A woman in her seventies was putting hers down on the jetty in front of the outer pool and sat down on it. When she spotted Rosa, she raised her hand in greeting. Margrit was one of a group of women who came here every day in summer. After all these years, there was no need to make plans any more. Whoever arrived first simply saved a place for the others and opened up the terracotta-coloured parasols. Rosa sometimes had a short chat with them; she had got to know them through swimming and as a result of her work. The ladies had a special relationship with the animal world. They called the diving ducks Fridolin; every duck was a Fridolin. The swans, a little more distinguished, were called Henry. And so the ladies had often been the first to arrive when an animal got caught or lost somewhere in the baths. Usually they notified the maritime police, whose clientele included not only humans but also all the creatures that populated the lake and the city's rivers.

'Do you fancy a little something with that?' Margrit waved a bottle of herbal schnapps and pointed to Rosa's orange juice.

'Another time maybe, but thank you,' Rosa said.

Margrit dropped the bottle back in her bag, not without first taking a sip. Time had flowed through her heavy body and left behind veins, wrinkles, countless moles, and yet this body looked as if it were blooming in contented harmony, now that it no longer aspired to please anyone but only to serve its purpose. Rosa wondered when you actually began to be the person you wanted to be. Perhaps when you stood naked in front of a mirror and *really* liked what you saw?

Margrit balanced a clipboard, with several waxed macramé yarns attached to the clamp, on her evenly tanned legs. 'I'm actually working on a tapestry now, but it takes up so much space in my bag.'

Rosa watched for a while as she deftly wove wooden beads into the bracelet.

'I taught myself,' Margrit said with undeniable pride. She told Rosa how she had learnt the art of knotting with a video tutorial.

'The knots don't seem to be any different from sailing knots,' Rosa said. As she watched Margrit, a thought flashed through her mind. 'Perhaps I will try it too, sometime.'

'You know where to find me,' Margrit replied. Then she rummaged through her beach bag and pulled out some already finished bracelets from among a bottle of sun cream, a pack of cigarettes and a bag of stale bread for the birds. 'Make a wish!' she said, and tied one round Rosa's wrist. In the past, Rosa had always wished for good health, the key to all other wishes. But today something else was more important.

'When the knot comes undone by itself, then the wish will come true, but only if you wished wisely.' Margrit winked at her, making countless wrinkles spread round her eyes.

When Rosa left the baths, the first thing she did was to type a message to Tom. He would almost certainly do her the favour she was asking for.

'S O THAT WAS the missing piece of the puzzle.'
Martin started running the surveillance video. The footage showed a montage of various camera locations by the lake. Rosa, who had headed straight to police headquarters from her swim, looked at the date. They were from the day of the performance of *Turandot*. They all showed the same couple. She almost didn't recognize the doctor. This was down to the perspective as well as the changed context. The young woman in the off-the-shoulder evening dress lent his tall figure additional glamour.

'How did you find the recordings?'

'The visit to Alina Orlov's flat-share yesterday was quite helpful,' Martin said. 'Even though, according to her flatmate, she is off for a few days in the mountains doing digital detox.'

'So she was the one with the falsely registered phone number from Duckburg?' Rosa asked.

'Looks like it, yes. We haven't been able to pick up a signal from the number since Tuesday near Zillis. One of Alina's flatmates remembers Jansen well. Apparently, in the weeks and months before his death, he was a regular, silent, night guest in the property,' Martin said with a glint in his eye.

Then he was serious again: 'He was also there on the evening of Opera for Everyone. According to the flatmate, Alina had planned on going to the mountains with Jansen. But shortly beforehand, he broke up with her, out of the blue.'

'Were you able to take a closer look at the villa?'

'Yes, but Alina Orlov's fingerprints don't match those found on the *Venus*. Our colleagues from the forensic institute checked. There were a few love letters from Jansen, but nothing that really helps, except perhaps the fact that she is actually quite active in the Open Science Movement.'

'And what does Ryser say about that?' Rosa asked.

'She's put out a search warrant on Alina Orlov. We have to assume that she was the last person to see Jansen alive.' Martin sank down on the office chair.

'What I don't understand,' said Rosa, looking at the frozen image of Jansen with one arm protectively round his companion, 'is why he—clearly head over heels in love—met up with someone from an escort agency the evening before going to the opera with his lover?'

Martin crumpled up the pizza delivery flyer and threw it towards the basketball hoop mounted on the wall.

'Maybe he was worried that she was going to dump him? Maybe he was afraid to commit? No idea. I can't think when my stomach is empty. Shall we go and grab a bite to eat?'

Rosa didn't answer straight away. She should have refused, but there was a really good street barbecue nearby...

The Palestine Grill made food based on traditional family recipes, which was reflected in long queues in front of the food truck at lunchtime. When Rosa and Martin reached the colourful truck, the big rush was already over. Minutes later they sat down at an empty table with a filled flatbread and a bottle of ice-cold rose lemonade each. Just a couple of metres away, the Prime Tower glass skyscraper was soaring upwards, smooth and green. On some days, reaching for the clouds, it dissected the sky into mirrored facets.

'The most important ingredient for a *sabich* is the hardest one to get,' Rosa said as she dabbed her fingers on a paper napkin. 'For the sauce, you need sour picked mangoes, with a mysterious mix of spices that have to include turmeric and fenugreek.' She wanted to go on and tell Martin that the amba sauce originally came from India, but is now used throughout the Middle East and that, if necessary, it could be replaced with mango chutney. But when she saw how much he relished biting into his pitta bread filled with fried aubergines, hummus, salad, potatoes, boiled egg, coriander and pickled cucumber, she decided to do the same.

'You asked earlier why Jansen met with Tonya despite him having a date with his lover shortly afterwards.' Martin pensively stirred the sugar in his espresso, for which they had taken the lift to the top floor of the skyscraper. The restaurant there offered the maximum contrast to the street food below: polished chessboard floors, moss-green velvet chairs, a gleaming golden bar and, of course, a panoramic view of the city, which from up here looked like a very complex model railway landscape. 'Perhaps the meeting on the *Venus* had a business connection?' he asked. 'I am pretty certain that Tonya knows more than she's letting on. She is covering for someone. It must have something to do with the phone calls between Neaira and the start-up.'

Rosa, who was scribbling in her notebook, looked up. She had traced the line of the Uetliberg with her pencil, despite its contours being so familiar to her that she could have done it from memory. 'I'm not sure. I am more suspicious of the other women.'

She wrote three names in front of the landscape: *Ellie Jansen. Marie Duval. Alina Orlov.* And then circled the first.

'Experience shows,' Martin said, following her train of thought, 'that the strongest emotions often arise in the family home. Ellie Jansen was not only betrayed, she also feared for her livelihood. She would have had to give up the house, maybe go back to working as a psychiatric nurse... Now she is not only getting a widow's pension, but probably also a handsome inheritance. From that point of view, she benefits the most from her husband's death.'

'But one thing speaks against it,' Rosa pointed out. 'She would have robbed the children of their father. What mother would do that?'

'I can think of a few,' Martin replied. 'But yes, that's a good point. As a woman, you can easily destroy a man in court in this country with a divorce. If you are unscrupulous enough. And she's worked hard at that.'

'Well, yes,' Rosa answered. 'According to the new legislation, women are actually expected to support themselves again even after long-term marriages. But the courts don't really implement this yet. Especially when the income differences are as high as they are here.'

Rosa drew a circle around the second name. 'Marie Duval… the investigations came at the worst possible time for her, just before she was about to list CRISPR-Cure on the stock exchange.'

'On the other hand, if the company is successful in the long term, Duval will have to share less, provided the heirs agree to be bought out. Moritz Jansen didn't leave a will. Now his widow and sons inherit their compulsory share and that's worth quite a bit.' Martin scraped out his cup. 'How can someone of Jansen's age and position not make a will? Especially in the middle of a divorce.'

'Fear? Denial?' Rosa shrugged her shoulders. 'He probably preferred dealing with the beginning of life rather than its end… maybe he just didn't get round to it. By the way, I took a look at the growth figures for biotech companies. They are gigantic.'

'Duval doesn't give me the impression that she is overly concerned with money.'

'Except that money stands for recognition,' Rosa said. 'But in her circles, you get that from somewhere else. A few years ago, Duval and Jansen published a scientific paper together. They were searching for a way to use the gene scissors more precisely. They picked this up again in the start-up…'

'We should have another look at what exactly they have been working on,' Martin suggested. 'Especially with regard to the IPO. There was an article in the paper yesterday about Duval…'

Rosa nodded as she circled the last name. 'Alina Orlov, the woman who got everything started. What could Jansen have had that was of interest to her? Did she perhaps want to use him as an entry ticket to Duval's research?'

'Perhaps we will know more tomorrow,' Martin said. 'I have signed us up for a workshop led by Alina's brother Yuri. Field research mark two in the Hackerspace Chaos Computer Club. You should look forward to it—you are going to meet your genome there.'

32

Y OU WOULDN'T COME ACROSS the former central laundry by chance; it was surrounded by high fences. Where once fifty tons of laundry were washed every day, artists, musicians, hobby gardeners, urbanists and utopians as well as activists, enthusiasts and doers now gathered, as it said on a joint leaflet on the noticeboard. Over the past decades, every generation in the city had had its own temporary use for the factory, in which the collective memory lived on. Rosa remembered the parties in the former paint factory, where you could only access the dance floor via a steep slide. And she remembered the self-built pool in the basement.

'Shall we?' Martin asked. He seemed to be in a particularly good mood today. A meeting was being held on a loading ramp at the entrance. The platform was covered with Persian carpets, and the flea market sofas created a corner shop atmosphere that was at odds with the sparseness of the empty factory building behind. The people who came and went here wore knee socks with sports shorts from the 1980s, colourful dungarees and overalls. But to Rosa the clothes seemed less about function and more about affiliation. She looked down at herself, her plain shirt, her denim skirt, her well-worn favourite trainers... and suddenly felt boring or old or both.

The lab was on the top floor, but Rosa and Martin didn't take the lift. The walls of the stairwell were covered with graffiti and slogans. Rosa could make out the key symbol of the Open Science Movement. They stopped in front of a particularly elaborate image. *Where is your vulva?* was written in curved letters. People had drawn various answers to the question and glued them on the wall: vulvas in figs, vulvas that turned into open eyes, looking into the cosmos, flower vulvas, heart vulvas, crumpled labia, inner and outer, vulvas with colour gradation, pastel vulvas and shell vulvas.

'Did you know there was a queer-feminist community in the bio-hacker scene?' asked Martin, who had obviously come well prepared for the visit to the Hackerspace.

'I only know the stories that were in the press a few years ago,' Rosa replied. 'People who set up their own labs in kitchens, cellars or garages and analysed and perhaps even manipulated genes there. But it's actually quite logical that there is an interest in doing things for oneself and working on gender selection without expensive medical treatment.'

The door to the laboratory was wide open. Pieces of cut glass hung from the grids of the neon tubes that covered the ceiling, casting refracted light in rainbow colours across the room. *CRISPR-baby, Occupy Biology, Biology of the 99 per cent* was written on a glass case in the entrance. In the case was a plastic doll and a signed manifesto:

We are prepared to explore and to cross borders. We are prepared to accept things that lie outside whatever the 'majority' of people would call 'normal'.

We define our own standards.

The words in the glass case made Rosa shudder. Martin, on the other hand, seemed to have a soft spot for biopunks and DIY biologists.

'This reminds me of the first computer hackers, crazy nerds, without whom it would never have been possible to democratize technology,' he said.

'I am not sure you can compare it,' Rosa said. 'I once had a seminar at university about the 'Gentlemen Scientists' of past centuries. Amateur butterfly collectors and recreational botanists, including Darwin. I think they were actually the predecessors of today's biopunks.'

They headed over to the bar, where cloudy liquid was bubbling in various vases. Water kefir, Rosa immediately deduced, since she herself kept kefir cultures to make flavoured lemonade.

'With the crucial difference that today's experiments no longer involve just plants and animals, but humans too,' Martin said, looking critically at the water kefir Rosa had poured for him. 'In principle, all you need are some materials from the pharmacy, some equipment that you can buy cheaply online, and a couple of freely accessible instructions and videos. Then you can do things that were previously only possible in a professional laboratory. For example, working on your own genome.'

He took a sip of the water kefir and grimaced. Rosa couldn't blame him.

'They haven't done the second fermentation,' she said. For that you add sugar, chopped fruit or herbs, thyme for example. I'll make you a proper kefir lemonade sometime.'

'Oh, there's no rush,' Martin replied, as a connecting door to the rear part of the laboratory opened.

'Right, here we go then,' Rosa said, with a sinking feeling in her stomach that wasn't from the water kefir.

'Don't worry, it's completely safe,' Yuri Orlov said, adding more salt. They were sitting at a long table together with seven other workshop participants; each of them had a disposable plastic cup in front of them. In it: their own saliva, some washing up liquid, contact lens cleaning fluid and a pinch of salt.

'You could actually down it in one,' Yuri said, and looked around the group, most of whom were young adults. Rosa had recognized him immediately—even though he had replaced his rhinestone-decorated face mask with an ordinary hygiene mask and tied his hair back in a bun.

The experiment was supposed to make their own DNA visible in a shot glass. Beforehand, they had sucked on lemon halves to stimulate their saliva production. 'Cells from our oral mucosa are swimming in the saliva. In principle, the cells are nothing but small fat bubbles,' Yuri continued. 'We have dissolved them with a little washing-up liquid. Or rather, their outer membrane. And that now reveals what lies underneath.'

Then he demonstrated how, very carefully, they should allow a small amount of rum to run down the rim of the shot glass until a clear dark-brown layer covered the cloudy mixture.

Rosa held her breath for a moment when white threads started snaking up to the surface of the brown rum. Although these looked the same in all the participants' glasses, they were as unique as the people themselves. It almost seemed indecent to Rosa when she fished the gooey threads out of the cup with a toothpick; they held nothing less than her innermost blueprint.

'We've had the federal police here for a visit too,' said Yuri Orlov, pointing to a laminated certificate hanging on the lab's refrigerator: *Biosafety officer, safety level 1*.

After Martin had explained the reason for their visit, Yuri pulled out some tobacco and roll-up papers from his lab coat, which he wore over a shirt with a cacti print on it. 'Can we go outside for a moment?'

Yuri led them through an emergency exit on to a fire escape that ran up the outside wall of the factory.

'Right from the start I didn't understand what she wanted from that reproduction guy...' he said as he sat down on the concrete steps. The silver creole earrings in his earlobes glimmered against the light. He started rolling himself a cigarette.

'You knew Moritz Jansen?' Rosa asked.

'I didn't know him. He sometimes picked Alina up at the lab. He never came in, but just waited in the stairwell. I suppose my sister is in trouble?' Yuri brought the roll-up to his lips to moisten the glue with his tongue, revealing geometric tattoos on his lower arm. 'I guess the question is superfluous when the crime squad pay you a visit.'

'When did you last see your sister?' Rosa asked.

'Sunday before last. She borrowed a sleeping bag from me for her nature trip to the mountains.'

'It would be in your sister's interest to get in touch with us as soon as possible. She was the last person to see Moritz Jansen alive. Her disappearance raises some questions.'

'That reminds me,' Yuri said, 'a few weeks ago, Alina's former professor came here. She's not exactly my sister's biggest fan since the event with the college computer.' He grinned and lit the cigarette. 'Anyway, the two of them had such a massive row that the entire lab took to their heels.'

'So you didn't hear what it was about?'

'Afterwards, Alina just said that Duval could get stuffed. At the time, I thought it was about the Open Science Movement. That the professor was probably afraid that Alina would leak some more papers. Maybe she was pissed off that she had taken her lover?'

33

S INCE THE PARKING SPOTS had been removed on
Zähringerplatz, the neighbourhood had found a new
lease of life. Benches beckoned in the shade of the trees and
boules balls clattered across the gravel, followed by exclamations and applause when they got close to the wooden target
ball. People drank their aperitifs on the edge of the fountain,
their bare legs in the cold water. They usually took along
one or two spare glasses from home just in case someone
they knew happened to be passing.

'Rosa!' Richi called out delightedly. 'We hardly ever see
you any more. There's *no way* you are sneaking past us.' He
fished for the bottle of white wine that was floating in the water
fountain to keep it cool. 'Basil Spritz, my current favourite.'

'And my favourite filler plant,' Rosa said, 'that is close
to blackmail.' She had discovered the aromatto variety at
the market a few years ago. Since then she had appreciated
its uncomplicated growth and even more the pretty blossoms that filled the gaps between the taller plants such as
coneflower and angel's trumpet so well. Richi had boiled
the dark-green marbled leaves into a syrup, which he was
now spooning out of a jam jar.

'*Santé!*' he said, after refilling the glasses with white wine and mineral water, and clinked glasses with Rosa. All over the square, people were eating from platters of cold snacks they had brought with them as if they were all guests at a big summer party. They were probably also enjoying the calm before the storm ahead of the street parade that was taking place the next day. The biggest techno party in the world flooded the city with hundreds of thousands of revellers every year. Afterwards, it was best not to swim in the lake for a few days and to wait until the next rain had washed the urine from the alleys and parks.

Shortly afterwards they were joined by Erik, who had come straight from the clinic. While enquiring whether Rosa was still interested in the research on the genetic scissors, he rolled up his trouser legs and sat down next to them with a sigh of relief.

Rosa tried some of the baked goat's cheese that Richi offered her, accompanied by figs from the Black Garden and roasted walnuts. Then she told them about the shot glass experiment. 'They are convinced that they are making the world a better place with bytes and genes. In the past, you needed things like fusion reactors or plutonium to do cutting-edge research. Now all you need is knowledge, information and code.'

Richi held up the wine bottle questioningly.

'I'm sorry,' Rosa said. 'I am probably boring you. This is certainly not something you want to hear about after work.'

'On the contrary,' Erik replied. 'It's extremely interesting. The genetic code has emerged from a war between viruses and bacteria that has been going on for billions of years. Meanwhile almost all living beings have their own DNA. And with CRISPR, we hold something like the key to editing all life in our hands. The system no longer functions like a pair of scissors, it is much more precise in its application. More like a Swiss pocketknife.'

'I don't want to spoil your fun,' Richi said. 'But you do realize what you can do with technology like that? And I am not saying that just because I'm playing Mobius…'

An hour later, they parted company outside the antique furniture shop. Feather boas, records and life-size contorting dolls with colourful wigs adorned the shop window this time. Rosa went out back to the garden and picked up one of the watering cans filled with sun-warmed water.

It was true what Richi said: people were good at finding out new things, but bad at weighing up the consequences. This common thread ran through history: tools always became weapons, and the first nuclear chain reaction did not simply usher in a new age of energy but also led to catastrophes.

Fine rivulets flowed through the flower beds before they seeped into the earth. The notion that by interfering with the germline, changes in the human genome would be stored forever frightened Rosa. Didn't it belong to everyone? Didn't this mess up the natural equilibrium forever? For all she knew, this had probably already happened. Perhaps Erik was right and it would be possible to correct an unjust genetic fate in the future. But she was firmly convinced that nature would always find new ways to leave room for chance or fate.

That reminded her! She must get round to taking a look through her medical record because her confidence in technology had waned noticeably in the past few days. She quickly refilled the watering cans at the tap and hurried into the house.

It was already growing dark outside when Rosa swiped through the files on her tablet, the cold glow illuminating her face. The eggs had been handed over to the university clinic, as a receipt proved. Rosa pushed the device aside.

She had everything she needed for a portion of summer rolls in the fridge. Shortly afterwards, with practised movements, she was filling the soaked rice leaves with yellow peppers, cucumber, mint leaves, spring onions, romaine lettuce and crispy tofu. When she was almost done, she realized that she had forgotten to add the crushed peanuts. She quickly put the heavy mortar on the table, which caused the pestle to slip out. It landed on the tablet with a threatening crack.

Swearing quietly, Rosa wiped away the nut crumbs and checked that the device was still working. Alba's name suddenly lit up and reminded Rosa that she had been hurriedly clicking aside the photos of her newborn nephew for days now. She wanted to do the same with her sister's medical

record, but the first few sentences were already jumping out at her.

When she finished reading, Rosa stared at her reflection on the dark screen. If the image had been sharper, she would have seen the deep furrows on her brow. She had also lost her appetite.

Dazed, she fetched a box from her writing desk upstairs. She put it down. The wooden floor under the futon creaked as she turned to the side and opened the memory box. One look at the yellowed photograph and it was back in a flash: the gleam of the Christmas lights and the smell of yellow candle wax and cinnamon sticks, beneath which lay a tension that could only be suppressed for a brief moment by the crackling of paper as presents were unwrapped. Alba, no more than a bundle in her mother's arms, her thumb between her half-opened lips. Rosa and her sister Valentina, kneeling in front of the Christmas tree on the floor, in itchy woollen tights, little checked dresses and patent-leather shoes. Far behind them in the shadow of the tree: their father.

It must have been during the time when Vinzenz seemed increasingly absent. He moved further and further to the edge in the photos, as if he wanted to slip out of his life unnoticed. Perhaps as a child Rosa had already sensed his conflict between responsibility and dullness. At least she remembered the feeling of distance. When she observed other families or was invited to a friend's house for dinner, she felt something that was missing in her own home. For a long time—her mother's covert remarks had played their part—she had blamed herself. Because she was not enough. Not grateful enough. Too sensitive...

The sudden buzzing of her phone jolted her from her thoughts.

Fifteen minutes later she got into Martin's car, which was waiting with the engine running at the Neumarkt bus stop. 'We've had some news,' he said. They turned right at the Kunsthaus in the direction of Bellevue. Fisler from Forensics had found out that Jansen had been injected with ketamine. The ketamine levels in his blood were incredibly high, which made him suspicious. He then carried out further tests and examined the corpse again, meticulously. 'And lo and behold, there was a puncture mark on the leg. Now Ryser has her murder case.'

'And where are we headed now?'

'To Ellie Jansen.' The traffic light switched to green, and Martin put his foot down. 'Now that we're actually investigating a murder, the telephone data suddenly became available very quickly. The widow was not only in Wildhaus on the Friday, she was also on the infamous corner in Niederdorf.'

When they arrived at the bungalow between the vineyards where Ellie Jansen lived, there was already a Forensics and a local police patrol car outside. Inside it looked similar to their last visit, only this time there was a different reason for the mess.

'I think she needs to come up with a really good explanation for this,' Ryser said. She held up a plastic bag containing a glass vial. 'Clinically pure ketamine, as used for pain management in emergency medicine or for anaesthetizing patients with low blood pressure... There is more in the medicine cabinet. A lot more.'

34

T HE BASS POUNDED from the Rosenhof, a final test for the party that was about to begin. It was one of many that would be held on the city's public squares while the love-mobiles moved around the lake. The Limmat flashed at the end of the narrow alleys. There was one bar after another there today, interrupted only by stages and floors filled with booming music, and a visit to the toilet cost two francs. At the back of the old town, in the streets behind the Zähringerplatz, the city cleaners were preparing for the upcoming battle with bins the size of shipping containers.

Rosa quickly pulled the print-off of Alba's medical records from her backpack. She had just over an hour before Ellie Jansen, who was now in custody, was questioned.

The retired doctor had kind eyes. Rosa wondered how many people he had had to give a fatal diagnosis to in his career. They were sitting at one of the round high tables at Manon. Twice a month the restaurant hosted the Café Med. The flyer read: *Straight talk, no jargon.* Here relatives and patients could get a free second opinion over coffee and cake. BRCA2-gene mutation—the name on the medical file sounded like science fiction. Rosa had searched online, but she still didn't know what the situation was regarding heredity.

'Essentially, the report says that your sister decided against pregnancy because one of her parents died from a serious form of cancer.' The doctor put the file down.

Wait a moment, Rosa thought. That can't be. Her parents were alive and kicking, so that must mean…

'So you are saying that my sister didn't want to get pregnant herself because the condition is hereditary?' Rosa asked quickly to conceal her confusion. The blood rushed in her ears. It must mean that Vinzenz was not Alba's biological father.

'That's what it says here at least,' the doctor said. 'But it's not a death sentence by any means. You and I and everyone else is born with this gene. But in some very rare cases, it also comes with a mutation. If you carry this, it may make a form of cancer more likely.'

'More likely? So it is not certain?' Rosa asked.

'The mutation has a fifty per cent chance of being passed on,' the doctor said. 'But genes don't determine at which point in time the disease will break out, or whether it will break out at all, or what sort of course it will take.'

Rosa listened as he explained that external factors such as alcohol, nicotine and other cellular toxins played at least as important a role. Just like the air you breathed. The feelings you had. Simply the whole life you lived.

'Imagine a marble lying on the top of a mountain,' the doctor said. 'When it rolls down the mountain, it has the choice between all the various valleys and chasms. It gains momentum and perhaps jumps out of its track because of a tiny little stone and lands somewhere completely different. And it's exactly those tiny little things that dictate the paths in our lives and ultimately make us what we are.'

Rosa sketched a serpentine ski run on her notepad with just a few strokes, where marbles instead of cars rolled down the mountain. And she asked herself whether she was as free as she had always believed. *You can become anything you want to be.* The promise had hovered over her youth like the Spice Girls' anthem 'Wannabe'. But the older she got and the longer the period of time she could look back on, the more clearly Rosa saw that she herself was limiting her choices, so that they no longer extended beyond a certain range. Trapped in the unchanging patterns that provided security. She wasn't sure whether her marble would ever be able to move to a different valley. Or even to a different serpentine run.

35

'I LIVED IN A PERMANENT state of distress before,' Ellie Jansen said. 'When you don't know in the morning how you are going to get through the day. Always, always this bloody emptiness. Every day, every morning, all over again. Do you see?'

Her gaze wandered across the interrogation room, past Martin and Rosa, to the window. The art school opposite was deserted on this Saturday morning. Then the widow looked back at the bottle of nasal spray, which lay in a labelled plastic bag on the table in front of her.

'It was just an enormous gift for me.'

She described endless attempts at therapy with ineffective antidepressants. And how she found out about a new approach from a former colleague at the psychiatric clinic: considerable success had been achieved with minimal doses of ketamine for depression. 'I always had the spray in my handbag. You can have the composition checked. Then you'll see that I am telling you the truth.' Ellie Jansen pushed the small bottle away from her. 'It wasn't about the hallucinogenic effect or the intoxication, nor was it about separating my body from my mind, although that might have helped me. No, I just wanted to calm down for a few hours.'

'Why didn't you seek medical help for the treatment?' Martin asked.

'I did. But here, unlike in America, research is still in its infancy. It will be ages before the therapy is approved. I don't have that time!' She jutted out her chin. 'Besides, I am a professional.'

'So you used the medical ketamine from the ampoules in your bathroom cabinet to micro-dose yourself?'

'If that's what you want to call it…'

'And why did you omit to tell us that you made a trip to Zurich during your spa treatment?'

'That was a mistake. I should have told you from the start that I was in Niederdorf for a short while that day.' Ellie Jansen dabbed at her sweaty brow with the sleeve of her blouse. 'But to be honest, I was scared. Just scared of losing my sons.' Her voice wavered. She swallowed a few times.

'Everything fell into place so well. No one had noticed my absence at the spa. It was so simple to just let things happen. You probably wouldn't have believed me if I told you that I went straight back to Wildhaus after standing outside a locked door on Häringstrasse.'

What were you doing in Neaira?' Rosa asked.

'I wanted to talk to… someone, get some proof, anything that might have helped me in court with the divorce.'

'And why did you decide to visit the establishment on that day of all days?'

'An anonymous tip-off…' Ellie Jansen slipped her wedding ring, which had become too big for her, off one finger and on to another.

'That's enough,' Martin said, exasperated. 'Who gave you the tip-off?'

'I had to promise not to say anything, otherwise…' she began. 'Although it doesn't matter now, you know about the ketamine thing.' Ellie Jansen took a deep breath in and then out. 'The tip-off came from Marie Duval, Moritz's business partner.'

36

ALBA HAD ALWAYS looked a few years younger than she actually was. 'That's because you were born in a leap year,' they always used to joke whenever their little sister had to show her ID to get a beer. Strictly speaking, she only had a birthday every four years. It was only after the age of twenty that her rather round face acquired the contours that made her beautiful in an unobtrusive way. Alba's large, wide-set eyes with their long eyelashes reinforced her childlike appearance and were able to conceal her stubborn nature.

Rosa, who had to take on responsibility from a young age, often used to get annoyed at the carelessness with which Alba moved within the family dynamic. Her sister was still as carefree as a child running barefoot across warm tarmac. Floating, almost weightless, with no knowledge of the burden that time would place on her shoulders. But now Rosa saw her sister differently.

'Family comes first, no question,' Martin said when she asked for a couple of hours off after the interrogation that had lasted until noon. Ellie Jansen had been taken back to the remand centre.

The matter of the micro-dosing sounded odd, but in all its oddness believable too, at least in Rosa's opinion. Martin didn't buy the widow's strange coincidences, but Ryser had explicitly instructed him to follow other leads as well. What if someone knew that Ellie Jansen kept the ketamine ampoules at home and had chosen the substance as the murder weapon for that very reason?

The analysis of a hair sample from the widow would quickly show whether she had been feeding them a line about her own consumption or not.

Rosa set off to visit her sister. Away from the booming, pumping hive that the city centre had become just before the parade began. Ever since Rosa had read the medical file, she had felt... yes, how did she actually feel? She seemed to have grasped the situation rationally, but everything else in her was numb.

She almost felt as if she were cycling through someone else's life as she rode past the stubbly fields on which heavy ears of corn had waved in the wind just a short while ago. It already smelt of countryside. Of wild chamomile and sandy paths.

'Mum and newborn *must* carry on sleeping,' Rosa insisted with a smile when Alba opened the front door on tiptoe, wanting to invite her in. Instead, Rosa suggested that she lend her sister a hand with the apple harvest. Normally Alba and Katrin offered nature education weeks for schoolchildren in the summer, but this year they wanted to concentrate on their own offspring.

'The trees are still bearing fruit regardless,' Alba said, pointing to the orchards surrounding the old farm. 'I think even more than usual. Particularly the early varieties.'

The familiar sound of feet kicking a ball came from the playing fields. A buzzing sound came from the ivy that covered the barn door. In the semi-darkness of the barn, there was a musty smell of farm earth and stored potatoes. In one corner boxes were laid out with picked apples, which they now carried outside to the well. Alba had already set up the mechanical juicer there. They chopped up the apples and put them into fine-meshed nets. Rosa silently thought about how best to begin. She reckoned that Alba would immediately clam up. Even as a child, she had cut out sad passages from picture books and hidden them under the bed, as if this were the way to get rid of monstrous threats. But it was no good, the question had to be asked.

'I only met him shortly before he died. He wrote to me to tell me that he was my biological father. A few weeks later, on All Saints' Day fourteen years ago, he passed away,' Alba said in a calm voice, much too calm, Rosa thought. 'At the time, no one knew that his illness might be hereditary. A genetic mutation that has a fifty-fifty chance of being passed on to every new child, in every generation. I only found out later.'

'How did he find you?'

'I got this letter, in straggly handwriting, every letter pointing in a different direction. But it rearranged my life.'

'And Josefa?'

'One look at her face and I knew it was true.'

'You should have had the right to meet him sooner!'

'What would that have changed?'

Instead of answering, Rosa put one of the bulging cloth bags into the press and turned the ratchet until the juice flowed into the wooden bucket. How would she and Valentina have reacted if they had learnt that Alba was 'only' their half-sister? As a child, she probably would have preferred to live with a lie than to be even more out of the ordinary than they already were.

'And Vinzenz has bottled that up ever since?' Rosa asked.

'I'm sure that he at least suspects it. Yes, perhaps he knew about the affair,' Alba said. 'In a way, I was even glad because I had an explanation for why he never really let me get close to him. The time in the club and working at the bar helped me. And then, later, Katrin. The whole thing only came up again when we decided to start a family.'

'Did you get tested?' Rosa asked instead.

'I wanted to at first.' Alba looked into the barn. White feathers hung like a fan on the wooden wall and trembled in the draught. Gifts from a peacock they had rescued from an amusement park that had closed down. 'I almost went mad. *Ball on red. Ball on black.* It's like roulette, only that this time your life is at stake. Just suppose that the ball had landed on red. Then I wouldn't know any more than the fact that I have an increased risk of developing a certain type of cancer because of a mutation. A type of cancer that spreads very aggressively. Which you can barely test for. And that almost always gets discovered so late that it ends up being fatal.'

Rosa felt the hairs on her forearms stand up when Alba said: 'As long as nothing changes, I won't get tested. I wouldn't be able to live with the certainty. This way I can at least imagine the glass is half full.'

'So that's why you decided against a pregnancy?'

'Eventually, yes, even though Jansen offered to put us in a trial group of a new gene therapy that might solve the problem.'

'What did he do?' Rosa sat up straight and looked her sister in the eye. 'Try and remember exactly what it was he said. But I have to know everything.' Then she switched on the recording function of her phone.

37

T HE TELEPHONE on the table was ringing again. Sophie
Laroux took such a deep breath that her nostrils flared.
She closed her eyes, counted to ten and switched the sound off.

Then she crossed her arms and went over to the window.
The heat of the day was slowly fading, even though the city
still seemed to be bubbling with people. The parade by the
lake was nearing its finale. Kilian had urgently advised her
to make a statement only in his presence, better still to say
nothing until she was up before the judge. But she wasn't
sure what his assessment would be if he knew the full story.
If he knew about the girls from the red-light area, about
the egg collections, the pregnancies. And the tests carried
out in the laboratory.

All along, she had been sure that she was doing the
right thing. Not to mention the fact that she had been paid
well. Really well. For the women, it meant going a few days
without the smell of semen, which adhered invisibly to their
fingers and didn't disappear in the shower. Instead, they
could recover from the abortions in a hotel with full board.

Sophie Laroux went to a sideboard by the entrance
and pulled a silver case of cigarillos out of the drawer. For

a moment, she felt as if she were not alone. She listened carefully, then shook her head. When this was all over, she desperately needed another holiday. A few weeks in Paris would be good. No, further away. Perhaps Bangkok?

She opened the window and blew the acrid smoke of the cigarillo outside, where the decibels crackled. All she had done was make the connections. An extra service, so to speak, for her long-standing client Moritz Jansen.

But by the time Marie Duval got involved, she had become more cautious. Perhaps it was best for her to come clean. Tonya would sing like the little birds in the aviary by the lake if the police increased the pressure a bit more. It would be better if she got in there first…

Suddenly Sophie Laroux felt a jolt, then her feet lost their footing. Her body lost its centre of gravity. She tipped forwards. She plummeted in terror. Sophie Laroux wanted to scream. But her throat remained silent.

38

'THE SIMILARITIES are almost bizarre,' Rosa remarked. She had come directly from Alba's farm to Häringstrasse, which was blocked off with red and white tape, and where several police cars had already gathered. Sophie Laroux had fallen out of the same window as the punter had under mysterious circumstances several years before. But she had been lucky. Rosa looked out of the window, four storeys down to the ground. If the city's service skip container hadn't been standing open, filled with plastic bottles that had been collected from the parade, then it would have all been over for Sophie Laroux. But instead she was in hospital with several broken bones and a skull fracture, waiting to be operated on. 'I don't suppose she is fit enough to be interviewed?' Rosa asked.

'No chance...' Martin said, and opened the door. The forensics team with their heavy suitcases were already standing in the hallway of the attic flat. 'Ryser has put two security men outside her room, just in case. After everything that's happened, it probably makes sense. At least until we know more.'

'What about the cameras?' Rosa asked pointing to the book-sized screens embedded in the wall next to the doorbell.

'It seems that it doesn't have a recording function.' Martin moved a step aside to make room for his colleagues from Forensics. 'Shall we go and grab a drink somewhere instead of standing in the way here?' he asked Rosa.

'You mean strictly professional?'

'Coffee rather than gin and tonic. I promise.'

'By the way, I really need to tell you about my visit to my sister,' Rosa said. 'You won't believe it…'

'That's crazy!' Martin turned in a circle with his hands up to make it clear that he didn't just mean the wash house or the ancient ash tree or the Black Garden, but simply *everything*. There had been so much going on at Zähringerplatz that Rosa's ears had started ringing just from walking past. The parade was over, and people were passing the time at the numerous street parties until the evening parties began at nightfall. Rosa had suggested that they hold their meeting back at her house, because the backyard, which was in the eye of the storm so to speak, was surprisingly peaceful today.

'When I moved in, there were just a couple of measly bushes here,' Rosa said, spooning coffee powder into the Bialetti. Then she told him about the legend of the Black Garden.

A bell founder once lived here. He had a wife from the Orient, as beautiful as the camellias, lilies and date palms that grew around the fountain in his courtyard. The garden of paradise was supposed to make his wife forget that she was locked up because the bell founder, a very jealous type, kept her under lock and key behind high walls. No one ever got to see her face. But whenever a child was born in Niederdorf or someone died, a silent servant would bring velvety fruits, colourful flower bouquets or opulent herb wreaths from the Black Garden—all year round, always fresh.

Rumours of magic and sorcery spread like the unusual fragrances that sometimes wafted over the walls, scents of rosewood and musk, neroli and cinnamon. Because he could no longer put up with not knowing, a squire whose property bordered the bell founder's had a high tower built. But when he finally made it over the wall and down the other side, he found—nothing.

No trace of the bell founder, nor of his wife. No dress. No body. Not even a tiny bone. Only a black, burnt wasteland.

'And now you are guarding the secret of the Black Garden?' Martin asked, rubbing a sprig of rosemary between his fingers.

Rosa laughed. 'I read the crystal drops that form on the leaves every morning.'

'Then maybe I shouldn't ask what they say about me,' Martin said with a smile.

At that, Rosa quickly opened the laptop. 'We need to set up a genetic comparison of the traces in Neaira with all those who are under investigation…' She typed noisily. 'Are there any other surveillance cameras nearby?'

'As far as I know, no. Residents have repeatedly demanded them, but it always led to loud protests in opposition, resulting in everything staying as it was,' Martin said, and sat down opposite her. 'What happened with your sister?'

For the next quarter of an hour, Rosa told him all about how her youngest nephew had come into being. Of course she left out all the elements that had to do with her own egg-freezing. Then she played him Alba's recording.

'You mean they actually interfered with the germline? And used the embryos?' Martin asked incredulously.

'At least my sister believes she was made such an offer.'

'If that's really true…' Martin whistled between his teeth, 'that would be an unimaginable scandal.'

Rosa entered a few terms in the search engine. In most countries, experiments on human embryos were forbidden. And where they were not forbidden, the embryos had to be destroyed after a few weeks. 'But Duval wouldn't have much to fear, at least not from a legal perspective,' she said. 'The Reproduction Act envisages a prison sentence of up to three years—or a fine, regardless of how many embryos are involved, even if several were edited…'

'I'm no scientist,' Martin said, 'but isn't that almost an invitation to do it?'

'If Duval really did carry out such experiments,' Rosa replied, 'then she must have needed a lot of eggs in the last few years. And the best place to get them is where no one asks about them. For example, in the sex trade.'

'That would also explain why Sophie Laroux had to disappear,' Marin combined.

'The coffee!' Rosa jumped up and rushed into the kitchen, where the burning-hot Bialetti was angrily bubbling over. She put a jug of cold milk on the tray and added some ginger biscuits and two of Stella's cups. When she turned round, she almost collided with Martin.

'Can I do anything?' he asked.

Rosa just about managed to stabilize the little jug before she handed Martin the tray. As he carried it out into the garden, she noticed that the tips of his ears were at least as red as hers.

39

FOR SOME IT WAS A VICTORY for life when the crowd jumped around the decorated floats and the streets around the lake, transformed into an enormous dancing body. A body, bare, then made up and dressed up, partying against mortality. Only there to kiss, drink and love.

But in the bright light of the morning, it became clear who had the most staying power. The last remaining ravers trotted towards the station with smeared make-up, dragging rumpled tulle through the dirt. Others took shelter at one of the numerous day parties and waited for nightfall to postpone the reality check for as long as possible.

Alina Orlov, on the other hand, got on the tram in front of the main station and headed straight home. When she had seen the unanswered calls from her flatmate, she immediately knew that something must have happened. After Alina listened to her voicemails, she took the first train back to Zurich. With a head full of questions and panic in her stomach.

Three hours later she was sitting in an interview room at police headquarters, adjusting her glasses with their photochromic lenses. 'At first I just thought he'd popped to the baker's...'

'And you didn't think something might have happened?' Martin's voice sounded softer than during the previous interviews. Even wearing cut-off jeans with a loose man's shirt over them, Alina seemed to have a certain effect on him.

'I felt uneasy about the overly hasty separation from his wife from the start,' she explained.

'Why? The divorce proceedings were already under way.'

'There was still too much energy in it all. It seemed to me as if he didn't want to let his wife go. Even thought she was fighting him, or perhaps because of that.' Alina needed a moment to stop her bottom lip trembling. 'I was sure he had gone back to her.'

'Did you use drugs together that evening?' Rosa asked, and refilled their filter coffee.

'Some...' Alina sat up right. 'But nothing compared to what is taken in the clubs every weekend.'

'What did you *take*?'

'MDMA crystal dissolved in champagne, if you really want to know.'

'No ketamine?'

'Definitely not. You only take that when nothing else touches the sides any more.'

'And I suppose you slept through the search for a missing person the next day? You live right by the lake...'

'Exactly. That's how I know there is always something going on there.'

'When did you hear about Moritz Jansen's death?'

'Yesterday evening. My flatmate had already left me a message on Wednesday after the police came round. But I had switched my phone off just before I set off just under two weeks ago. Digital detox. Maybe you've heard of it.'

'And what about last Tuesday?' Martin asked. 'Your phone was located in Zillis.'

Alina looked perplexed. 'Ah, yes, now I remember.' She smiled, slightly embarrassed. 'I had lost my way and had to search for the area to get my bearings. But I switched the phone off immediately afterwards.'

'The number isn't even registered to your name,' Rosa said.

'So the tech giants can track my every move? You can report me for it. I would do the same again any time.' Alina turned to Martin. 'But I did actually want to help you.' She pulled something out of her jeans. 'Do you always leave such a mess behind when you search places?'

'Sometimes we can't help it,' Martin grumbled.

'At least it helped me to find a note that Moritz left for me with a globe on it. The evening before his death,' Alina paused, 'we talked about a picture that hangs on my wall.' She handed Martin a memory stick. 'It was hidden in the frame. It contains information about a project called…'

'Human Nature,' Martin finished her sentence for her.

Alina Orlov looked at him in surprise. 'The memory stick only seems to contain part of the study, and the participants are anonymized. But there is enough information there to interest the press. There is even a sub-folder in which the results are summarized in layman's terms.'

'So was Moritz Jansen intending to reveal them?'

'I certainly didn't know anything about it...' Alina said. 'The study describes a method of eliminating unwanted effects when using the gene scissors. Quite clever. The experiments were also successfully implemented on a small trial group.'

'You mean interventions into the germline?'

'That's exactly what I mean! But I would have to know all the results in order to judge that more precisely. But I am sure that Duval wants to keep those under wraps—patent protection...' Alina slipped her hands back in her pockets.

'What is your relationship to Marie Duval?'

'As good as can be expected with someone who got you kicked out of university out of fear of competition—and whose partner you took.'

'Do you think that Marie Duval killed Moritz Jansen? What did you argue about a few weeks ago?'

Alina raised an eyebrow and tapped the memory stick. 'It all makes sense now. Back then in the Hackerspace, I didn't really understand what she wanted from me. I thought it had something to do with my relationship with Moritz. I knew they had been an item once. He made a strange allusion that night by the lake. That the man-eating Princess Turandot also represented Puccini's own inability to be with the woman he loved.' She took a deep breath and then exhaled slowly. 'I thought he was referring to his ex-wife. But I was probably wrong. Marie Duval would probably rather die than expose her CRISPR method to the public. And that's exactly what Moritz wanted to do.'

40

'THEORETICALLY, we are only limited by our imagination,' said Marie Duval, putting on a pair of disposable gloves. 'Everything is faster, easier and cheaper with
the new technology.' Sitting on a high chair, she wheeled
past the dry desk where the work was being carried out in
the lab. Following the conversation with Alina Orlov, Rosa
and Martin had immediately headed over to the start-up
offices. Although it was Sunday, they had found Marie Duval
at work. The lab was divided by transparent partitions that
had mathematical formulae and DNA ladders scribbled on
them. At the end of each work unit there was a separate
office in which to feed the results of the experiments into the
computer system. The shelves were piled high with all kinds
of plastic containers with different-coloured lids. Petri dishes.
Pipettes. And other equipment for which Rosa had no name.

'You really want to win the race at all costs, don't you?'
asked Martin, who was also wearing a white lab coat. It was
compulsory at this security level.

If he made Duval uncomfortable, she knew how to hide
it. She took her time. She calmly placed the sample in the
rotary module and started the shaking procedure.

'Normally, the professors in whose laboratory a discovery is made take all the credit. That's how it works in the science industry…' Duval explained how the CRISPR technology had been discovered by chance in an experiment with yoghurt cultures. It was reported on pig organs, which were adapted so that they could be implanted into humans. There were mosquitoes that were resistant to malaria and beagles whose muscle mass had been doubled.

'But if you change the genome of embryos,' Rosa interrupted, 'then the genetic changes not only affect the human in whom they took place, but also the generations that follow, correct?'

'You are alluding to the Chinese scientist who manipulated the twin girls with the HIV-positive mother? He shouldn't have done that, not without eliminating the unwanted effect.'

'And you can do that?'

Duval went over to one of the incubators that was kept at a constant 37 degrees, body temperature. She placed a petri dish under the microscope. 'See for yourself.'

Rosa bent over the device and recognized a jagged structure, almost like skin-coloured snow crystals.

'Those are cancer cells. They keep growing. Faster and faster. But with the genetic scissors, we were able to eliminate them.'

'Have you ever implanted modified eggs into a human?'

'You mean do I approve of research on embryos? What do you think—is it worse or less bad than using laboratory animals?' Duval asked, stowing the samples from the rotary module in a fridge beneath the dry desk.

'We had a visit from Alina Orlov this morning.'

When Martin mentioned her name, a barely perceptible jolt went through the scientist's body.

'Did you ask her where she was the night Jansen died?'

'Alina's answer was the same as yours: at home. Only she found a memory stick there belonging to Jansen with information on a project called Human Nature. Is that what you argued about with her at the factory?'

'Rubbish!' Duval waved it off. 'We started Human Nature years ago. It fills the gap in research that can't be done at the university. The systems are too slow, too much basic research. After my time at Berkeley, I wanted to set up something of my own. I happened to run into Moritz again at a symposium in the Bernese Oberland. Shortly afterwards, he joined CRISPR-Cure.'

'And the argument with Alina?' Rosa asked again, determined not to let herself be distracted.

'She was here at the start-up a few weeks ago with Moritz. I caught her rummaging through my desk. A folder with documents disappeared.' She cleared the petri dishes with the cancer cells away. 'The folder turned up again shortly afterwards.'

'Might that have been the information regarding the eggs taken from sex workers that you use for your research?' Martin asked.

Duval turned to face him. 'Sometimes you have to know how to help yourself,' she said. 'Such experiments are allowed in other countries. If the results are groundbreaking enough, then everyone who knows anything about it will still want to read the research paper.'

'Where were you yesterday early evening?' Rosa interjected. 'That was when Sophie Laroux fell from the fourth floor on Häringstrasse, or should I say she was thrown?'

'Oh my goodness, how awful! I was here in my office, as my business partner will be able to confirm. You already know Ravi Kathoon. I barely had anything to do with Laroux. Moritz made the contact—and he also dealt with the egg collection. My job only began here in the laboratory when the nitrogen tanks arrived.'

'There are documents on the memory stick that suggest that you also implanted embryos with manipulated DNA in a trial group.'

'Is that right?' Marie Duval opened the glass door with her key card and stepped out of the laboratory. Rosa and Martin followed her.

Their footsteps echoed down the wide corridor that led to Duval's office. She unlocked her computer. 'Go ahead. Make up your own minds. Here is all the information on Human Nature.'

Martin took a cursory glance at the computer. Of course Duval knew that he could neither read nor properly interpret the results.

'Why did you contact his wife the day before Moritz Jansen died?' he asked, and turned away from the screen.

'She had contacted me several times before.'

'Was she jealous? After all, you and Moritz Jansen were a couple once.'

'I thought it might be good if she saw for herself what Moritz was up to. It probably helped her to let him go.' While Duval recounted the long conversations she had allegedly had with Ellie Jansen, Rosa took a look around the office.

The almost empty desk with its shiny surface was as inconspicuous as the utensils neatly lined up on it: a stapler, non-coloured highlighters, Post-it notes.

A steel locker stood in the corner. Rosa pulled open the door. Clothes in thin, transparent garment covers hung on a rail; they had obviously come straight from the dry-cleaner. The locker looked as if the professor regularly travelled a great deal. The only personal detail was a photo pinned to the inside of the steel door. It showed the scientist when she was younger, on a rock with her diving goggles pushed up, with the gleaming ocean behind her.

'That was on the Cyclades. Great for diving,' said Marie Duval, who had appeared behind Rosa. 'We all carry a tiny bit of primordial sea inside us. There are barely two fluids that resemble each other's chemical composition more than human blood and seawater. At the beginning of our lives, when we are floating in the amniotic sac, our earliest physical characteristics resemble those of fish.'

'Do you still dive regularly?' Rosa asked.

'Not for a long time. But I miss it. The feeling when the blood flows into the middle of the body from the extremities and the heart beats more slowly. Slower and slower until all the senses are dulled and there is only a deep feeling of peace.'

Rosa, too, knew this world away from reality with undulating water plants and shimmering mists of plankton in a deep, dark blue, with black darkness underneath that swallows everything...

Duval's voice brought her back to the spartan office.

'I now know that free-diving has more to do with research than I once thought. No compromises. The goal always ahead of you. Never think of the way back.'

Duval closed the locker with a jerk and removed the key. 'Is there anything else you need?' She turned towards the exit. 'I have a lot to do.'

Rosa reached for her bag, which she had placed on the floor next to the desk. As she did so, she noticed a thick strand of cable that ran along the legs of the desk and was tied with a knot that she had encountered very recently in a different location. Unnoticed, she pulled out her phone.

Shortly afterwards, they said goodbye at the reception desk, where explanatory videos were still playing on a continuous loop.

41

T HERE WERE ONLY three bakeries in the world that
knew the original recipe for the cream pastries. The
monks are said to have stirred the custard made of egg yolks
day and night in their secret workshop in Lisbon. People
in Zurich who wanted to satisfy their travel lust tried to get
their hands on one of the twenty *pastéis de Bélem* that Pablo's
wife Aurelia baked every day. Rosa pressed the earphone in
a little deeper so that she would hear if Martin called. He
was holding the fort in an inconspicuously parked patrol
car close to Marie Duval's Tesla, while another colleague in
civilian clothes was stationed outside the lecture hall. This is
how it had been all week. With an occasional detour to Zug.
Ryser had ordered a stake-out right away after the evening
visit to the lab. And as Marie Duval's lecture today lasted
until shortly before noon, Rosa had taken the opportunity
to stretch her legs at the foot of the university hill and stop
by Pablo's grocery shop on Neumarkt.

She placed a paper cup under the coffee machine, which
was easily accessible in the wine corner. Then she pressed the
button and watched the fragrant trickle. Then she repeated
the procedure.

'One per person is not enough,' Rosa said with a laugh when she ordered a *pastéis* from the large tray behind the counter. Aurelia said all she needed was flour, sugar, eggs, milk and butter. No cream. It wasn't rocket science. Just the right temperature and the right mixing ratio. But the little cakes had to contain a pinch of magic. They tasted like a morning spent in Lisbon. Rosa paid. On the wall behind the cash register was an impressive selection of spices from all over the world. Her gaze rested on a tub of salt flakes and its image of a mermaid's billowing hair decorated with starfish. She quickly tucked the bag under her arm and grabbed the coffee cups. Her farewell greeting was swallowed by the tinkling of the bells on the shop door.

'Sophie Laroux is still in intensive care.' Martin blew into the coffee cup, but then decided to return it to the drinks holder in the patrol car. 'If only we could speak to her… Forensics have tried to simulate the fall. If someone actually pushed her out of the window, it would have been easily done. No one saw the fall itself, but we have a witness in the house opposite who remembers seeing Laroux at the window, smoking, with her arms propped up on the window sill. If you sneak up on someone from behind and resolutely lift up their legs… bang!'

He hit the steering wheel with the flat of his hand and the noise made Rosa flinch. 'You hardly need any strength—you just need the right moment. The rest is done by gravity. And then she's been silenced.'

'Come to think about it, Jansen's murder bears the same signature,' Rosa said, wiping a crumb of puff pastry from the back of her hand without taking her eyes off the narrow alley. Stone steps led steeply up the slope, the shortest way to get to the university district. It was still quiet for now.

'What if,' she let her thoughts run free, 'someone, for example, an experienced free-diver, surprises her business partner, who is already wobbly on his feet. She arranges to meet him—perhaps on a motor yacht where they have met several times before. But on that morning, she dives towards him unnoticed as he paddles out on a small dinghy. She waits until the water is deep enough. She dives under the dinghy, capsizes it and... bang!'

Now Rosa slammed her hand on the dashboard above the glove compartment and noticed with quiet satisfaction that Martin also flinched. 'Just like with the fall from the window: all she needs is the help of the water, and the balance of power between her and Jansen on land is dissolved.'

Martin's eyes gleamed as he spun out the thought. 'She had already lured him on to the *Venus* in the afternoon on a pretext. After the murder, she drives the body to the deepest part of the lake on the yacht. There she sinks it. She leaves the engine running to make it look like an accident. She arranges the drugs around the used glasses from the afternoon and dives back to shore unnoticed. There she changes her clothes and starts on time with the Ironpeople, giving her an alibi.' Martin whistled through his teeth. 'An almost perfect murder. But why does she make it so complicated?

Couldn't she have just left him floating by the boathouse until someone found him?'

Rosa furrowed her brow. 'Maybe she wanted to buy some time? Two full days passed between Jansen's death and the discovery of his body. Or to throw suspicion on Sophie Laroux? A feeling came over me yesterday in Duval's office, but I couldn't put it together. Not yet.' Rosa folded the empty paper bag from Pablo's shop on her knees. 'It was only today when I was fetching the coffees that the sketch of the mermaid on the salt tub caught my eye.'

Martin looked at her sceptically.

'Forget it.' She made a dismissive gesture. 'But what if Duval wanted to give him a kind death? Underwater, in the blue-green light. An encounter with a magical figure, ancient and gruesome. A death almost like an enactment.'

Martin scrunched up his nose. 'Don't you think you're reading too much into it? Just because of a past affair? Besides, she's a scientist and not a professor of German...'

'Don't underestimate what a narcissistic piqued lover is capable of,' she replied.

Martin drummed his fingers on the steering wheel.

But Rosa would not be deterred: 'This way, Duval was able to create his last memory and associate the end of his life with hers.'

'Sounds a bit too lofty to me,' Martin said.

Annoyed, Rosa lowered the side window so as to fill the space between them with fresh air, along with the voices of the students coming down the steps in ever larger groups.

'I am sure that every murder takes place in a certain world. It has to be logical within this world. The laws that apply within it are what makes it happen. This can also be a world that you maybe can't imagine—although you are welcome to swap "world" with "psyche". We don't understand what Duval is doing in her lab either.'

'Yes, but if you want to make a murder look like an accident, then it's a bit like lying: stay as close as possible to the truth, and then people are more likely to believe you. Or in our case: stay as close as possible to your victim's habits and routines.' Martin thought for a moment. 'If we transfer this to Duval, this would mean that she took into account what Jansen did that evening with his lover anyway and then took it a bit further.'

'Exactly! Do you want to know why I'm so sure?' Rosa didn't wait for his reply. She removed the bracelet that she'd been given in the bathing pool by Margrit from her wrist. She looped it twice round a Biro. 'The constrictor knot is highly unusual. Just like the butterfly knot or the timber hitch... I hadn't seen it for several years.' When the bracelet made a nice pretzel shape, she pulled on the two ends. 'Done.' Rosa held the pen up in the air. 'A genuine constrictor knot.' She told Martin about her visit to Jansen's boathouse and then opened the photo archive on her phone. 'I took this picture yesterday in Duval's office.'

Martin frowned at the sight of the cable strand held by a thick cord. He enlarged the image. 'That could actually be right.'

Rosa scrolled down the photos until she got to the image that Tom had sent her a few days ago after she'd asked him to take another look at the fertility clinic's boathouse. It showed the rope on the front of the dinghy. It had the same knot.

'It's all circumstantial, I know, I know…' Rosa raised her hands before Martin could point out that this would not be enough to be considered evidence. 'But circumstantial evidence can be put together to form a picture. Whether it's enough for a conviction is not up to us, thankfully. Tom took the rope to the forensic institute. We'll see if we can't find some of Duval's DNA on it…'

Martin interrupted: 'Isn't that her over there? Why didn't they tell us that the lecture finished early?'

Sure enough, the red rear lights of Duval's Tesla came on.

'Right, let's go then,' said Martin, and followed the car, keeping an appropriate distance. A light drizzle began when they arrived at the top of Hirschengraben and turned off in the direction of Central. They followed the Tesla along the Limmat, westwards past the tapering headland behind the National Museum.

Traffic was still flowing smoothly out of town, but this could change abruptly on a Friday afternoon as soon as the commuters finished work.

'So we can eliminate two possible destinations already,' Martin said as they left the city heading towards Bern. 'She is definitely not going home to Kilchberg and not to Zug either. Where is she going?'

42

Y OU COULD EASILY have overlooked the inconspicuous steel door on the far left of the wall. The entrance to this Swiss Fort Knox for data security was in keeping with the country's tradition of discreetly and unobtrusively hiding valuable things. In this case, it was data treasure that the mountain not only watched over; it also protected the whirring servers from overheating with an underground glacial lake.

Martin and Rosa had left the motorway at Spiez, which led past the Niesen. In the pouring rain they had followed the Tesla through the green valley with its rugged rock faces. On arrival at the data fortress's car park, they had seen Marie Duval disappear behind the steel door before they properly realized what they were looking at. Between fields and farms, just two kilometres from the upmarket ski resort of Gstaad, the digital assets of companies from all over the world, from bitcoin pioneers to government regulators, were embedded and stored deep in the rock, in an old army bunker.

'I know about secret numbered bank accounts, but this is something else…' Martin said.

Rosa looked through her backpack for something to eat, but found nothing except some peppermint drops.

'I bet Duval has the Human Nature results stashed here.'

'And if she has,' Rosa said. 'it will be impossible to get permission from our colleagues in Bern to obtain access.' She put one of the drops in her mouth.

'There's no need, she's come back out.'

Martin pointed to a figure walking hurriedly along the damp grey wall. Duval had put on a rain jacket; it must be chilly inside the mountain. She was carrying her handbag under her coat, pressed tightly against her body.

'That's enough,' Martin said. He opened the driver's door. 'Let's arrest her.'

'Wait!' Rosa pulled his arm. 'Isn't it better to find out what she's planning instead of arresting her and then not having any evidence?'

As they drove back through the valley, Martin began to cut the narrow bends more sharply than necessary. In some places, wet rocks leant out over the road. Time and again they were overtaken by infernally rattling motorbikes. Rosa was relieved when they reached Lake Brienz, where cloud shadows flitted across the turquoise glacier water, which was given its colour by tiny sediments. The road wound along the shore, past villages with wooden chalets.

'Damn!' Martin slammed on the brakes. A tractor pulled out in front of them. A liquid that looked suspiciously like fertilizer was dripping from the trailer. 'I can't see her any more. She's gone.'

Rosa tried to look past the tractor, without success.

There was no sign of the Tesla. When, with spinning tyres, they overtook the tractor at the next best spot Rosa sent a quick prayer to heaven. For lack of alternatives, they simply continued on the same road, past a military airfield where a fighter jet was landing with a roar, all the way to the end, where the Aare squeezed into a deep, narrow valley.

'Gotcha!' said Rosa, half to the tablet she was balancing on her knees to locate Duval's phone, half to Martin. Then she pointed to a sign pointing in the direction of Schattenhalb. 'That's the way up.'

43

WHEN ROSA PUSHED her way into the carriage, the departure signal had already sounded. The full funicular, which bore a certain resemblance to the Polybahn, moved off with a groan. Cowbells tinkled on the fields. Rosa could see Marie Duval, who was standing right at the front of the platform.

Soon there was a rushing sound, which grew louder and louder and finally drowned out all other noises as the train went past the first of the seven waterfall cascades. The Reichenbach Falls thundered down into the valley with such force that water rose again in the form of a veiled mist which the wind now blew over towards them. Rosa crossed her damp arms and glanced nervously at her watch.

During busy times like this, the two trains that passed each other halfway ran almost constantly. She hoped that Martin would make the next one. She had spotted Duval in front of the ticket booth below when two coaches had cut off their path. So Rosa had spontaneously jumped out of the car.

A few minutes later they reached the small upper station building, which was perched on an artificial plateau on the steep cliff. Rosa pushed her way through the crowds towards the exit. The saris of Indian tourists sparkled in the sun, which broke through the clouds and conjured up countless rainbow reflections in the spray. Louis Vuitton bags were quickly slung over forearms and dark sunglasses were put on. Barely anyone wore the right footwear for the path across the slippery steps that led to the waterfall.

Marie Duval was already overtaking a few walkers. The pale skin above Rosa's knee started to pinch, as if the scar indicated not only a change in the weather but also danger. The incessant swirling and roaring of the water made Rosa feel dizzy. She tried to call Martin, but it went straight to voicemail.

While she left him a message, Rosa also began the climb through the forest, which was so damp and dark that the trees on the weather side carried a thick fur of moss. She followed Duval at a distance. She kept having to swerve round people who had stopped to take photographs of the natural spectacle. Suddenly she saw the viewing platform ahead of her—and Duval, who was walking towards the precipice, which was secured by barbed-wire fencing.

Rosa quickened her pace and overtook a couple of hikers, who made indignant noises. She started running. But the closer she got to the platform, the more everything around her blurred, as if a door to the past had been pushed open...

A block of flats in one of the outer districts where boys with bottles of vodka and switchblades went around the houses at night looking for brand-name jackets and shoes they could take off someone weaker or simply less cold-blooded. Where hopelessness stuck to the tarmac like the spit they gobbed on the ground. The neighbours had called the police in the early hours of the morning. There had been incidents of domestic violence in the family before. Rosa, still in training, had waited outside the block of flats while two colleagues rang the bell. A door to a balcony on the ground floor suddenly burst open. Neon lights on the ceiling. It smelt of hot fat, spicy curry—and blood. Without hesitating even for a second, Rosa jumped up the railing. Her footsteps sank in the artificial grass carpet laid out on the balcony. The man had his back to her, a smeared knife in his right hand. He held a woman in a headlock with the other arm. A nine-month belly bulged from beneath her dress. Rosa ducked down. She dodged the paper bags stuffed with empty cans and bottles. The woman had seen her. Silently she gasped for help. Rosa crept silently to the balcony door and pulled out her weapon. Just as she was about to overpower the man from behind, it happened. Her foot got tangled. A toy phone with a red receiver made a ringing sound, and then all Rosa saw was the man's bloodshot eyes as he turned in a flash. Then she heard herself scream as she threw herself at him. But it was too late...

The sound of the water hitting the rocks brought Rosa back. Spray rose up towards her like smoke in a burning house. Was Marie Duval planning on throwing herself down? Impossible. The precipice was enclosed by a fence. The scientist pulled a grey-black object from her handbag, hardly bigger than her hand. She held it out over the railing as if she had to test how it might feel to let go. The thing, whatever it might be, would hit the ground several hundred metres down and burst into a thousand pieces.

When she spotted Rosa, Duval jerked back. The waterfall roared threateningly from below. Rosa removed her weapon from its holster and approached cautiously.

'Give it to me,' she shouted out.

Duval's gaze darkened.

'Moritz would not have wanted you to destroy your joint project,' Rosa shouted against the noise. 'Not after everything you both sacrificed.'

Marie Duval took a few steps until the cliff wall was directly behind her, then she slumped down. When Rosa approached with her weapon drawn, she was mechanically swaying her body back and forth.

'No one can say I had any other choice,' she said, looking through Rosa. 'I had to free Moritz. Just like I had to use the embryos.' She pressed the grey-black object, a hard drive, against her body. 'Every one of my acts was unavoidable.'

The professor was trembling in her wet clothes, drenched by the waterfall. When Rosa was almost at her side, Duval leapt up and pushed her aside. She approached the fence that secured the precipice once more.

Rosa felt as if time was standing still.

She struggled to her feet. Duval was almost at the railing. At the last second, Rosa managed to grab her shoulder and pull her to the ground. The hard drive slithered across the slippery rock. As Rosa tried to grab it, she felt a thud. Then she lost consciousness.

44

'I HAD TO DO IT,' Marie Duval said with composure, despite the pulsating vein that protruded on her forehead. The scientist's face flickered across the screen into the prosecutor's office, where Ryser cracked her knuckles and tensely watched the event going on next door.

Duval was still wearing the dirty clothes; her handcuffed hands lay in front of her like dead animals. Apart from that, she was calm and collected. Nothing in her expression indicated that she had completely lost it a few hours earlier.

'I had to do it...' she said, 'because only I could do it, no one else. Do you have the slightest idea what the study means?' She eyed Martin contemptuously. His jeans, the white cotton shirt, the leather jacket that hung over the chair.

'Then why did you want to throw the hard drive into the Reichenbach Falls?' he asked, without responding to her provocation.

Her bottom lip pushed forwards slightly. 'Because I won't share the results of the study with these Open Science activists. If they want to play in the top league, then there is more to it than just hoisting a few flags.'

'You should be at home now,' Ryser admonished Rosa when she came into the room. The bruise on the back of her head was throbbing, but she had insisted on coming straight to Mühleweg after the village doctor in Meiringen had examined her. She squeezed another painkiller out of the packet and Ryser handed her a glass of tap water. The incident at the waterfall had ended reasonably well. While Martin, who had finally reached the top, had stuck to Duval's heels, a quick-thinking French tourist couple had not only taken care of Rosa but had also secured the object of desire.

'It doesn't look like she is going to confess again,' Rosa said, staring at the screen, where Martin was resting his elbows on the table and scratching his head.

'I didn't kill him,' Duval said, her eyes glazing over. It was frustrating.

Since Rosa hadn't been able to record the confession at the waterfall, it was looking like a purely circumstantial trial. The confession was worthless in court.

'Have you seen today's stock market news?' Ryser asked without looking away from the screen. 'Rumours have spread that a groundbreaking method of fighting cancer cells is about to be patented, and as a result the share prices of the companies in question have gone through the roof. Capital markets play by their own rules. It probably won't impress them much if it becomes public knowledge that we are opening criminal proceedings against Marie Duval.'

237

There was a knock on the door and a pale computer scientist, whom Rosa recognized from the house search in Zug, came into the room.

'Either someone has gone to a lot of trouble not to leave any traces,' he placed the hard drive on the table. 'Or this is the wrong item. There is nothing on here at all.'

'Someone must have beaten her to it...' Rosa slapped her hand on the table and immediately screwed up her face in pain. That was the final piece of evidence gone up in smoke.

It was late when Rosa and Martin walked dejectedly to Escher Wyss Square. Engines roared and laughter and excited voices filled the night, which was just beginning to pick up speed under the Hardbrücke. Rosa felt the bump on her head, which would probably trouble her for a few more days. But even Martin, who had apologized several times for arriving at the scene too late, looked pretty crumpled. What had it all been for?

Apart from a couple of illegal egg collections, for which Duval would get no more than a fine, they couldn't prove anything.

'Have you ever tried the sausage there?' Martin asked, stopping outside an illuminated restaurant with red and white awnings, with an oversized bratwurst enthroned on a pedestal in front of it.

'Don't the inspectors normally hit the sausage stand after they have solved the case?'

'Normally, yes,' Martin said. 'But this place has a currywurst with a sauce created by a Michelin-starred chef. It's your sort of thing, isn't it?'

'Yes, it is,' Rosa said, and joined Martin in the queue of hungry revellers.

'Not bad at all,' Rosa said a bit later as they sat next to each other at one of the tables on the pavement with their backs to the wall. She speared another piece of the vegan currywurst on to her fork and dipped it into the sauce, which was unique; it contained an ingredient she couldn't name. She could usually always identify ingredients, but she wasn't on form today.

Colleagues had often told her about cases in which the perpetrators had made a confession that could not be used formally. Rosa had tried to comfort them by telling them that this said nothing about the quality of their criminal work. But now she knew that this was a very weak consolation. Martin had tried all kinds of questioning to get Duval to confess a second time. He had put statements in a different context. He had sharpened them in the same way that headlines are sharpened to produce a scandalous front-page story. He had even bluffed at the end. To no avail.

Martin listlessly poked at his food. 'The only thing that produced anything like an emotion was the mention of Alina Orlov.'

Rosa still had the professor's voice in her ear. *Moritz was completely blinded, he treated Alina as if she were a precious pearl. But in truth she was a parasite, fat and shiny and without any merit of her own.* In fact, that had been the only moment when Rosa recognized something of the woman who had collapsed at the waterfall. Why did she hate her former student so much? This made Rosa think of something. 'The thing with the empty hard drive is very weird,' she said. 'We shouldn't give up too quickly.'

Then she explained her plan to Martin. As she spoke, his hand crept ever closer to hers, until they were almost touching.

'Yes, it's worth a try at least...' he said when she had finished. He took her hand. 'And perhaps, when all this is over, we should start again from the beginning.'

She looked at him in surprise. Before she could reply, his phone rang. 'It's Ryser,' he said and answered it.

His face suddenly lit up. Sophie Laroux had come out of the induced coma and was responsive. She was prepared to testify against Duval.

'The tide has turned,' he said gleefully. 'And the best thing about it: there are cameras in the Neaira office, a whole surveillance system to which only Laroux has access.'

45

One month later

THE RED NIGHT TRAIN pulled into the station with squealing brakes. Alina shouldered her backpack. It had been liberating to sort out her life, pack everything away, until only the bare essentials remained and she was not weighed down by the baggage of a life dictated by routine. The travellers scattered across the platform came together. There was an energy that smelt of hastily smoked cigarettes, spilt energy drinks and old coins.

Alina was fortunate: the mirrored train door, beeping nervously, opened half a metre away from her. She passed through the expensive sleeping carriages that were wallpapered with images of mountain ranges and in which narrow ladders led up to the bunk beds. Alina had only reserved a single aisle seat. After checking the reservation, she sat down on the empty seat next to it. She placed her backpack between her legs and in relief leant her head against the window, which cooled her cheek. She felt for the hard drive that she had hidden in a small bag beneath her clothes. The stakes had been high. When she realized that Moritz was on her side, it had been too late. She could probably have saved herself the trouble with Marie Duval. Exchanging the hard drive where she had discovered it. Fortunately, Duval hadn't even noticed what had happened, she had only missed the stupid folder afterwards. But the action had aroused her suspicion and set in motion a reaction that neither of them could interrupt or control. It just happened, like a chemical experiment.

Perhaps—no, it would certainly have been different if she had been able to trust Moritz from the start, but she hadn't been able to do that. Although she had fallen in love with him. Actually, she had never managed it. Like a deep-sea fish that develops an additional sense to survive in its surroundings without light below the twilight zone, she had learnt early on to get along without trust and only continue with things which she was able to control as much as possible—and which she could get out of in an emergency.

The door to the compartment was yanked open. A man entered; he smelt of sour milk. And he had a sour expression on his face too. When he took off his cap, thinning grey hair appeared. He held his ticket under her nose like evidence, at which they swapped places. Alina held her breath in disgust.

After all, she had had no choice other than to resort to radical methods. In fact, no one who walked through this world with their eyes half open did. A world in which flames leapt so high that they formed their own lightning bolts. A world that would soon be buried under tons of meltwater. They were heading at supersonic speed for a man-made concrete wall; and people had nothing better to do than to roast their full bellies on the Costa Brava. Or to go daft in their last years on cruise liners, with fun cocktails with little umbrellas and all-inclusive deals… but the time would come.

And she would be prepared. *Terra Nullius*, the no man's land in one of the loops of the Danube, had been forgotten after the war. No one had laid claim to it. Not the victors. Not the losers. Only she had done so. A new republic was born on the river that had previously divided people into top and a bottom, upper and lower classes.

Hundreds of thousands were already its digital citizens: Arab sheikhs, Montenegrin judges, bankers from Hong Kong and maharajas from India. On the river, which would give off a Caribbean atmosphere with its bright beaches when the Bahamas had long sunk below the flood markers, they would initially be living on houseboats and later in high-rise buildings made of wood, the building material of the future. A gigantic blockchain project and an international location for research, supplied by renewable energy. Research that would enable them to prepare for what was to come in the decades ahead.

The minibar trolley rumbled along the carpeted corridor. Alina, who had dozed off for a moment, stretched her tense neck muscles. The train had just passed Buchs, near the Austrian border. She pulled out her jumper and rolled it up to make a pillow. They would be arriving in Slovenia at about nine in the morning according to the timetable, where the others would be waiting for her in a camp. Hopefully they wouldn't be angry that she had already messed around with the hard drive.

Her brother would certainly know how to crack the code. And anyway, she was the one who had obtained the data.

If it really did hold the key to functioning genetic scissors, then they absolutely had to share this freely. Everyone needed to be able to access it. It might make it possible for humans to adapt to the threatening changes and to survive on Earth in the future.

The steady chugging of the rolling train calmed her thoughts, and she had almost dozed off again when she suddenly felt a hand at her shoulder.

Alina Orlov jerked up and gazed into the face of a customs officer. Behind him stood a male and a female police officer in civilian clothes. She had hoped never to see them again.

46

I T IS ALWAYS SAID that luck is fleeting. But it lasted at the vegetable market on Bürkliplatz. While the swans drifted in the waves that were gentle at this early hour, their long necks still tucked into their feathers, the market vendors were setting up around the bandstand in the middle of the square, once an elegant meeting place for the bourgeoisie, as they did every Friday morning.

Every move was practised, everyone knew what they had to do. Strings of light illuminated the scene. Every time, Rosa fell into a dreamlike state when she saw the abundance on offer, which was never sweeter than now, in September, the time of ripe fruit.

It was noticeably cooler at night now, but during the day, an autumn-golden sun cast long shadows. Rosa had already eaten something before she came here, because if she arrived with an empty stomach she always bought more than she actually needed, regardless of whether she had a shopping list or not.

Half an hour later, Rosa loaded a full basket into Stella's van, which she had borrowed for the day. After a short week's holiday, which Rosa had spent rowing and making chutney and jam, she was back to normal duties at Forellensteig. It was her turn to cook lunch today.

She had already layered the aubergine casserole in a dish: several layers of aubergine, passata, mozzarella and black olives. It was accompanied by cocotte bread that had been rising almost the entire day in the warmth, before being baked in a cast-iron pot until it was so crispy that you could hear the crust singing as it cooled. And of course, a large bowl of lettuce with nasturtium, whose orange blossoms shone at the top of the basket, was obligatory.

After getting into the van, the first thing Rosa did was to remove the vanilla-scented car freshener that was dangling from the rear-view mirror and place it in the glove compartment. It reminded her too much of the drive that had taken place just a few weeks ago but which felt like an eternity, after the procedure at Jansen's clinic. The fertility treatment would have to wait, at least for the time being. Instead she wanted to give herself and Martin enough time to find out what might happen.

Richi, though, saw this differently and had always encouraged her to clearly express her wish for a child, and to do so right from the start. Perhaps he was right, but initially she had to let the last few turbulent weeks sink in. Andrea Ryser would be opening the criminal proceedings in court in the coming days. They probably didn't have quite enough solid evidence in the murder case of Moritz Jansen for a criminal charge. Even if they had found traces of Duval's DNA on the constrictor knot on the dinghy, that did not prove that she had killed him. Sometimes Rosa wondered if the scene at the waterfall had actually happened. Her memory of it had faded just as the bump on her head had disappeared. The case against Duval for the attempted murder of Sophie Laroux was more promising.

Rosa hoped it would at least bring some satisfaction for Jansen's family if the alleged perpetrator was sentenced to a long prison term for a different offence. And she had no doubt that would happen, because Sophie Laroux's lawyer was leaving no legal stone unturned. Rosa was sure that Kilian Graf would not only get a conviction for Duval, but also handsome compensation for his client, who was still in the rehab clinic but on the road to recovery.

The *Venus* had also been released a few days ago now that the case was concluded. It was still moored at Forellensteig. The owner had picked it up, and was planning to rent it out to a surf school in the future.

Before Rosa began her shift at Forellensteig, she had to do something. She ran her hand gently across the small package wrapped in tissue paper on the passenger seat. A last remnant of the secured evidence that she no longer needed now.

Rosa stood at the railing of the ferry and gazed out of the rectangular side window. Behind it was the lake, a framed landscape with rippling waves and wooded lines, already covered in a soft autumn hue.

This time the pieces fell into place.

Alina Orlov would probably receive a fine and a suspended sentence for attempted destruction of evidence. Despite them being able to secure the hard drive with the results of the Human Nature trial from her, it was worthless in helping to solve the case. The hard drive was secured with a special mechanism: you only had a limited number of attempts to enter the correct combination of numbers. If the number was exceeded, the hard drive automatically destroyed its contents, a technology which had already cost many a bitcoin millionaire his fortune. Alina had tried to crack the code herself. In the end, all she had left was the hope that her brother and his programmer friends in Slovenia would manage it. She had overestimated them, and herself. But even the police expert hackers saw no chance of getting round the security mechanism. And so the hard drive had disappeared into the evidence room. Perhaps it would be possible to decrypt it in a few years when the technology had advanced further.

But first Marie Duval had to stand trial for the illegal intervention in the germline. Even if she hadn't retrieved the eggs herself, Ryser would demand the highest sentence. Either way, Duval would almost certainly not be returning to a laboratory for years to come.

Eillie Jansen was sitting with bent knees on the steps outside the bungalow. The veranda was packed with removal boxes. If she was surprised to see Rosa, she didn't let on.

'We found this on the boat,' Rosa said, handing her the jumper that had been hanging over the *Venus*'s swimming ladder that morning. 'The case is closed now. I thought you might like to have it.'

The hint of a smile flitted across Ellie Jansen's face. 'That's very thoughtful,' she said, and hugged the jumper as if she were greeting someone. 'Many thanks.'

'You are really doing it this time?' Rosa indicated towards the open front door, through which the removal men were coming and going.

Ellie Jansen nodded. '*Tabula rasa*, the house has been sold, as have the company shares and the surgery... did you hear about it?'

Rosa shook her head.

'After I found out what Duval had done, I immediately realized that we needed to get out of the start-up. It will take months to divide up the inheritance, but we have already sold the shares.' Her eyes glinted. 'And that was just *before* CRISPR-Cure crashed on the stock market.'

'Sometimes there is a justice that is above the law,' Rosa said, and thought of Duval's unusable confession. 'And what will you do now?'

'We are going to set up a charity that supports Open Science and the observance of ethical guidelines in research worldwide. In this way, I can at least continue what cost Moritz his life...'

Ellie Jansen pulled her scarf tighter round her narrow shoulders. 'Sometimes you think you'll never get over certain things in life. But maybe the opposite is true. Maybe the only constant in our lives is that we always have to start again. At least that's what we tell each other.'

She waved to the twins, who were just coming out of the house carrying boxes. They wore their baseball caps back to front so that you could see their faces.

Back at the harbour, Rosa didn't go directly to Stella's van under the plane trees, but sat down on the low steps by the water. Lost in thought, she picked up a dead piece of bark that a tree had cast off as it grew. She looked at the light patches on the trunk, at the new bark underneath and to the lake, above which the autumn sky stretched so wide and clear that the horizon was indistinguishable from the water. Then she pulled out her phone and asked Alba when she might meet her nephew.

AVAILABLE AND COMING SOON
FROM PUSHKIN VERTIGO

Jonathan Ames

You Were Never Really Here
A Man Named Doll
The Wheel of Doll

Simone Campos

Nothing Can Hurt You Now

Zijin Chen

Bad Kids

Maxine Mei-Fung Chung

The Eighth Girl

Candas Jane Dorsey

The Adventures of Isabel
What's the Matter with Mary Jane?

Margot Douaihy

Scorched Grace

Joey Hartstone

The Local

Seraina Kobler

Deep Dark Blue

Elizabeth Little

Pretty as a Picture

Jack Lutz

London in Black

Steven Maxwell

All Was Lost

Callum McSorley

Squeaky Clean

Louise Mey

The Second Woman

John Kåre Raake

The Ice

RV Raman

A Will to Kill
Grave Intentions
Praying Mantis

Paula Rodríguez

Urgent Matters

Nilanjana Roy

Black River

John Vercher

Three-Fifths
After the Lights Go Out

Emma Viskic

Resurrection Bay
And Fire Came Down
Darkness for Light
Those Who Perish

Yulia Yakovleva

Punishment of a Hunter
Death of the Red Rider